The Abyss is the Foundation of the Possible — Writing On & Through Film, 2007-2018

by M Kitchell

THE ABYSS IS THE FOUNDATION OF THE POSSIBLE

ISBN-13: 978-1-7335694-6-0
ISBN-10: 1-7335694-6-4

Cover design by Matthew Revert

Cover art by M Kitchell

www.apocalypse-party.com

CONTENTS

INTRODUCTION

In the age of the algorithm, shunted from product to product by the circular logic of mass user recommendation data by highly trained machines, I relish the unpredictability and surprise of human curation. Ad bars speculate on my needs based on half-heard conversations, and I'm told that preference correlation engines run faster than free will. And so I covet crafted lists and canons. Not those authoritative, official selections, with their predictably narrowed criteria, committee decisions, and bland anticipation of consensus (for almost mechanistically averaged results to rival any digital system), but the outside, the idiosyncratic, the deeply personal, the seemingly unjustifiable. These kinds of media menageries (I'm speaking mostly of film, but it could apply to any) are an invitation to new territories. A few steps through one of these doorways, and you may find that the path behind has vanished entirely. All at once you're somewhere new, disoriented but filled with anticipation. Possibilities beckon.

It was in search of such portals that, in early 2010, I fed the particular incantation "grandrieux ruiz zulawski" into an internet browser and was whisked away to a blog post from two days ealier. The author was veiled by a pseudonym. The list of films posted contained those three directors and sixty odd other selections I'd never seen at that point and often never heard of, moving freely between genre, art, and experimental film, a blurring of boundaries I was finding myself increasingly drawn towards. Still in the days before streaming services, often reliant on a brick and mortar video shop five blocks away with a lingering collection of VHS tapes among the DVDs, these weren't necessarily easy to find. But I was intrigued. Along with a few other such collections arranged by strangers, this became a set of guideposts for my viewing that year.

Beyond the list itself, now long superseded by others evolving into ever-more particular incarnations, it was the way that M Kitchell (for it was he) wrote about the films he sought out that drew me in. In the unaffected space afforded by blogging, he put down his thoughts with a conversational elegance guided less by perceived universal cinematic standards than by personal passion. A work had value outside of objective scales if it spoke to him in a certain way, generated images that he found resonance in. Yet, through these personal entry points, he often extracted something essential from films, popular or obscure, that might otherwise go overlooked. When I found that he also published more serious reviews on his own site, Esotika, my impression didn't really change. Even in a more distanced critical mode, he was clearly charting a deliriously subjective viewing space of his own, a triangulation of horror, desire, and avant-garde exploration.

This was a period when I was awash in new influences. Kitchell's was one among many, but he just kept turning up. Sometime that year, I realized I'd independently run into book reviews he'd written, then that he was publishing his own fiction, often at the border of poetry and other less definable territories. I hoped that the same tendencies I recognized in his film writing might come through here as well. I was not disappointed.

Paul Garrior in Jacques Riverrun's "The Abyss is the Foundation of the Possible" was first published, that same year just over a decade ago, in *No Colony 3*, a joint literary anthology edited by Blake Butler (soon to unveil *There Is No Year*) and Ken Baumann (a little later to release *Solip*). All three, Butler, Baumann, and Kitchell, would later create a singular collaborative text, *14 Dreams of Death*. Also included in *No Colony* were three other shorter novella-length chunks of text: an ode to CEOs, a harsh, reduced tale of brothers and dogs by Peter Markus, and a sixty-author exquisite corpse created as part of a Pushcart Prize nomination scheme. I don't think any scandal ensued from that nomination, but M Kitchell's closing section of the volume dominated my impression of it anyway. Even the covers, a doubled face vanishing into an analog grid of CRT video energy on the front, part of the same image superimposed over a magenta tail-light-glowed house in darkness on the back, were much more in tonal and thematic continuity with Kitchell's piece than anything else there. Of course, these images turned out to be drawn from his photography. Within, a series of his collages overlaid occult landforms and architectures with hazy bodies, in dialogue with the text. *No Colony 3* was an anthology, but it felt like framing for a specific event, Kitchell's longest sustained narrative in print up to that point.

The Abyss is the Foundation of the Possible is a formalist collage story about the vampiric pull of the filmed image (a theme excavated further here in Kitchell's piece on Ivan Zulueta's *Arrebato*), the creative process, and the human voids of isolation and loss. The narrative is conveyed through an alphabetical glossary of film concepts—often almost essayistic, but always subtly feeding into the central dramatic tensions—intercut with contextless dialogues between two lovers and archival film materials culled from a long search. It's a lost film narrative, but unlike so many other lost film narratives, the film at the center is neither an empty plot device, nor a cypher that allows access to the characters that the reader can't comprehend, nor over-defined into banality. The film's fascination holds unwavering even as it is approached, thus does the entire story. It's an absence, yes, but "Absence" is the first alphabetical entry in the central notebook. Here, absences exert an inexorable gravitational pull.

The accompanying film essays that follow this novella in the new volume all expand cogently on Kitchell's vision, often locating alienation and isolation in seemingly utilitarian genre fare of the 80s and early 90s, erotica from Japan's pink cinema or the bloody edges of outsider horror film. Desire borders desperation, beauty shimmers forth from abjection. There's been more of a movement to reevaluate such media in recent years—two essays here concern the work of Hisayasu Sato, who recently became the subject of both funding and a documentary from MIT's Sensory Ethnographic Lab, for instance – but Kitchell is less interested in reevaluation than in mapping the intrinsic qualities that have allowed, beyond audience assumptions, such films to exert a subtle power from their first appearance. Likewise, experimental film here is studied less for its intellectual or conceptual content (or, as in traditional film education, its meaning at the level of signs and symbols) but for its ability to generate atmosphere and affect. These serve as a vital short-circuit, building meaning at the level of the viewing experience without overreliance on analysis or context. In this way, they perform a comparably visceral function to genre film's direct manipulation of the viewer's autonomic responses.

But if the film writings offer more evidence for the ways in which horror, erotica, and experimental film all function in direct communication with the viewer, even on a subliminal level, this is also all right there in the central novella. With its nods to Zwartes, Gehr, Franco, Robbe-Grillet, Cavallone, Breillat, Grandrieux, Bataille, and Hamilton—recurring figures in the Kitchell media landscape—as well as a scene from the, at that time, completely lost *Hu-Man* (1975), the story could serve as a kind of unorthodox canon in itself, an invitation to follow these markers and dig deeper. But more than it needs any specific reference points, the novella is a catalogue of ways of thinking about and encountering the filmed image. *Paul Garrior in Jacques Riverrun's "The Abyss is the Foundation of the Possible"* is both an essay on personal narrative construction, its possibilities and powers, and a direct example of these effects in action. This is deeply experiential experimental storytelling. Even the layering of the film poster tagline in the title hints at the feeling that underlies and informs its precise construction, welling up through omissions and allusions. This early novella, which provides its own map to its reading many times over, could also, then, serve as a key to much of Kitchell's subsequent writing. Here, the narrative is circular and vaporous, and later experimental novels and interlinked collections often dissolve further into completely nonlinear storytelling. But the emphasis on experimentation less for its own pleasures (though they are many) than as direct channel to meaning and understanding remains as a throughline. Even when interrogating dislocation and desolation, the hazy, blinking filmed image, or its written simulacrum, forges connection.

—Nate Dorr

Paul Garrior in Jacques Riverrun's "The Abyss is the Foundation of the Possible"

"When I make a film, I shift into the state of fascination with an object, a thing, a fact, a look, a landscape, as though it were an engine where the holy were just about to explode."

—Pier Paolo Pasolini

"Again the image looks at me, the eyes of that image; and, again, the inconceivable space forms between us."

—Philippe Sollers, *The Park*

ABSENCE

Forgotten. Never in a position to be remembered. Can the affectation of one individual upon another be expressed in any sort of medium other than existence itself? Hypothesis: no. Experiment with the impossible.

There is something missing. Something is gone.

The rising sun. A bedroom (whose?). White walls absorb the light from outside. Everything starts from (with) a bedroom. Introduced asleep. (Someone else present.) A body stirring on the bed. Floating. (Medium shot cuts to close up.) Imprint of a body left on a mattress, complementing the body that remains. The confluence of shapes forms a whole. Smells haunt the air: remember. What happened last night. What happens every night. What is happening right now.

The body stirs again. (Camera pulls out, away.) Light decorates the room, everything. A man opens his eyes. Hands rub eyes, fall back to bed. He stands up, nude except for a pair of tight gray underwear. Tangential details to provide a context: ruffled sheets, bedroom eyes.

The room's shaded windows paint the man's torso with shadows. Colored difference opens a stage of symbols to be interpreted. Hiding under these symbols: skin. Hiding under this skin: scars. Were body hair shaven nothing would be visible. No physical manifestation of abandon.

His vacancy is what is left.

BURIED

Afraid of everything that's been lost. Everything covered up. The sense of disappearing—forever. Each individual experience is lost eventually. Ends, finished, over. Libraries burn down. Film reels rust, chemicals stain. Negatives fade.

Digging a hole six feet, a hundred feet, a thousand feet underground. Eventually there's nothing down there but earth.

Once there were secrets (?).

The answers: not the answers that anybody is looking for. Can't remember the last time, or the time before that. Lost in thought. Wait.

A photograph once told something. Became an experience, a sliding, push the incident to both sides. Even it out. No.

Lovers get lost to the earth. Another plane where things are better. Can we access this other plane? Something underground has the answer. Nothingness, (limitlessness), void. Inner experience places the character at the edge of this precipice. The practice of joy before death. When is this practice learned?

A body beneath sheets, beneath blankets, writhing: experiencing anguish. The orgasm as the moment of *this*. Films that exist already—nothing. The films don't already exist. Not in this way, a wholeness. A mode of experience.

A storyboard:

> A man has lost his lover.
> He sits in a dark, undefined space.
> Light from behind highlights the shape of his body.
> A whiteness violates this space, overtakes everything.
> The man is lost to the inoperative spectrum of light.
> A crashing, unending white noise violates his ears.
> He might be screaming but the spectator cannot be sure.
> A warm synthetic tone infiltrates the noise, takes over.
> The white dims, and the man returns to view.
> He is not crying, but he could start at any moment.
> *Something has happened.*

The film: being in itself. Erotic potential—

A photocopy of an article from an underground French magazine—*Ciné-Cauchemar*, June 1976—comes in the mail. More of a blurb than an article. A rough English translation is attached, scrawled in a hastily handwritten script on the back of an outdated catalog card from the Bibliothèque nationale de France:

> *"J. Riverrun is currently working on his new film. Photographs of the entire film reveals that it is not for everyone, but we can assure that the readers of this magazine will be treated. The film deals with a ring of sado-masochistic math geniuses, convinced that quantum mechanics offers another universe. The group removed outcasts and have attracted businesses to carry out experimental metaphysics. If this were not enough, the film is shot as a pornographic film, all male. Make sure to be a unique experience for all. Currently being shoot, release planning for early 1977."*

An image decorates the page next to the blurb, but nothing indicates if this image is related to the plot description.

CUBE

A generative container. Two dimensional geometry expanding into three dimensions. Movement, from sight to touch. Eyes to fingers. More evocative, in some respects.

Things to remember, potentialities: quantum mechanics. Lovecraft's *Dreams in the Witch-House*. Geometry as a route to a parallel world.

Image: Intersecting walls, dim light. A wide angle lens collapses the corner (three walls) into a flat geometric shape. Out of the intersection, a figure appears. Zoom out, the corner is revealed as part of a larger structure. An abstract representation of space.

The structure as something concrete; material. The structure as a stage within a void of primary color. Spectators on all four sides, positioned below the performance-space.

Consider the inversion of a box: conical, but not rounded. A pyramid, flat, extending once again towards the top of the space after approaching the center. A funnel, wide on both ends, but restricted in the middle. One pyramid upside down on top of another. Markings on the outside: could be inverted crosses, more likely just esoteric symbols.

A narrative can be found here: there are rooms in the structure, an entire system of life.

"It was the middle of the night when I watched it. It had to be a sixth or seventh generation dub, and for the first ten minutes I had no idea what was even on the screen. But in the dark of my bedroom—and I mean, I was half asleep, a little bit drunk—the vague outline of a body appeared. It was beautiful. I think at first it was just my mind filling in the blanks, but suddenly the tracking adjusted and I realized that what I saw wasn't just a shadow in darkness, that what I was looking at was actually perfect. I'd never seen anyone that beautiful before. He had to be about 45 at the time it was filmed, alone on a bed with what looked like white sheets. I can't say for sure because—like I said—the quality was shit and the colors were undoubtedly fucked up. With all the dirt picked up copy to copy, the film's abject lighting made his body glow. He was naked, of course. I mean, this was when I was trading for the weirdest porno tapes I could find—I wasn't picky if it was straight or gay or whatever—looking for something that was like nothing else. But this was really something special. It was so minimal, so bare. And he was so perfect. Like, I'm not sure if a total representation of my type even existed before I saw him, but this tape filled in all the blanks for me. He filled in all the blanks for me."

"Why are you telling me this."

"Because it was perfect, and it was beautiful. After I watched the tape I spent weeks trying to find out who he was—or just anything about him. Eventually I tracked down a guy in—where else—L.A. who had some info. I guess the guy on the tape was a model who had worked for Colt Studios when he was a little younger;—he's in that compilation, Best of Colt Films 7 or something—but this was later. Late 70s. Turns out it was the last thing he ever filmed. But what was really amazing to me was that

the scene I had seen was actual part of a larger whole. A feature length film that may or may not have even been finished. There was, supposedly, an actual fucking narrative surrounding it. The guy in LA told me that the director was a crackpot who had spent six years studying under Frans Zwartjes at the Dutch Film Academy, but he got tired of academia and moved to California to make porno. Really bat-shit stuff, but apparently really beautiful too. The scene I had was from his only feature length porn. The guy from the scene—who I was, and am, totally in love with—he was the star. It turns out that this guy, well, he died at the end of the scene. Probably drugs or something, it's not important because he was just an image anyway, but apparently he literally dies on film. My copy was sourced from an underground compilation of necro-fetish stuff. But I didn't care. Don't care. He was, is, beautiful."

DISCONNECTION

Potential story outline:

> A labyrinth of hallways enclosed within a cubic inversion. A man is alone. A fragment of text (an inter-title?) reveals that a manifestation of his lust—pure physical desire—is found at the opposite end of the maze (is there a way to depict this while avoiding narration or the textual introduction?). The two ends of the labyrinth are separated by both physical and metaphysical space. The man is physically strong, but as he moves through the maze, he begins to emotionally collapse. This dichotomy heightens his senses. He becomes almost preternatural in his tactile sensuality: his fingers rub the walls as he walks the endless corridors.
>
> As he progresses through the labyrinth, he becomes emotionally overwhelmed. The space around him begins to incorporate the intensity of his lust. The viewer, as well as our protagonist, is unaware of any progression or regression towards the Other, the goal. The man wildly hallucinates colors as his heightened tacto-sensuality finds him rubbing his hands over his own hard body. Tears roll down his cheeks, betraying his masculine visage, challenging the expectations of physicality.
>
> At the end of the film the man has yet to encounter

> his Other. The camera, swirling around the outside of the structure, refuses to give the viewer any indication of the status of the Other: the manifestation of our protagonist's lust is lost to the structure. But the goal has become irrelevant: the man collapses onto the ground, exhausted and beaten, and finds solace in solipsism. His own body becomes the locus of his pleasure: the Other becomes a moot point. At the moment of climax the structure dissolves around him. He is now floating in a void, smiling. All signs of exhaustion are gone.

There is no way to manifest this narrative, ontologically, aside from the medium of the motion picture. There is a clash of images, sounds, and lights that must come together to form the diegetic world imagined.

In the basement of a private collector's abandoned warehouse—the specifics of the warehouse unknown—an Italian 2-sheet is found for the film *The Abyss is the Foundation of the Possible*. Titled, in this instance, as *La Fine del l'impossibile*. Transliterated, this title becomes *The End of the Impossible*.

The only text, other than the title, is the following:

PAUL GARRIOR

REGIA: J. RIVERRUN

Undated, the poster depicts a man writhing in the center of a void, a harsh spectrum of colors (blue red pink purple) surrounding his body. Overexposed light hides whether the man is fully nude or not.

ENNUI

The man who is bored on screen is the man who represents desire. To encapsulate the endless repetition of the sex act—to represent the point where lust becomes mechanical—this is to reach a level of sexuality rarely matched. On screen the figure is, generally, trying too hard. To achieve a performance that would evoke a response, one must make the character, the image-man, the film-body, look like he is not trying at all.

No mindless screaming, no excess of vowels as the moment of climax comes. Desire, fulfillment: both entirely internal. Externalizations of the sexual act imply an interaction with the other, and to have a pornographic production that is successful (active), the figure must only interact with the viewer. A distanced interaction is lessened, of course, by the space between. Virtual space.

The man who is bored on screen represents forgetting, and this is what the spectator of the pornographic film seeks: an active forgetting. Film is inherently a passive medium unless doors are opening up, via visual signifiers, via the experience of watching the film itself. Directly addressing the audience is irritating when the viewer is watching, actively, as a voyeur. A direct address does nothing to remove passivity from an already comatose audience. It is a futile trick.

Perhaps it is best to aim for the same mental space that the viewer inhabits while watching the film. A languid body scrawled upon a bed. Eyes barely open, muscles still. Perhaps a yawn can inspire empathy. But if nothing happens the viewer has no reason to stay.

It is difficult to assume the viewer will not be pushed too far in either direction. Too far away from an active response, too far towards a passive response.

Consider the storyline suggested before: the man who desires his desire, wandering through corridors. Too much action in such a situation would violate the illusion of a necessary suspension of disbelief. The search must consist exclusively of desire: one cannot make an entire "event" out of wandering alone.

But how can a man walking—battling his ego, his own sense of worth, lusting after the unattainable—share the mental space of the same body lounging, bored, emanating physicality from a prostrate position on a bed? Hypothesis: The answer is structural. Develop a repetition, a sense of stillness through an editing of the progression. Reduce the act to a non-act. What it is to desire the act of desire: repetition.

"So, wait—that's all you found out about your perfect man? That he's dead and he starred in some degenerate director's magnum opus? I wouldn't think you'd give up that easily."

"Oh no, that's not it—I mean, I found out more about him. It was hard though, you know? I had to do some pretty stupid things, like—"

"Doesn't matter. Just tell me what you found out."

"The feature length film—for the record, it's production title was The Abyss is the Foundation of the Possible, or something—wasn't the only film that the director had made with this utterly perfect, undeniably hot, completely impossible man—"

"Hold on—did you ever find his name? Too many adjectives for me to focus here."

"Oh yeah, yeah: Paul Garrior. But when he worked with Colt Films he was always credited as Ledermeister. I mean, at least I think his name is Paul Garrior. I've seen it spelled as "Gerrior" too. Like I said, I've never actually seen him credited in his later work, but some website—"Bear Roots Oral History"—says that that's Ledermeister's real name. But, what I'm trying to tell you is that this wild Abyss film wasn't the only thing Garrior had made with crazy-director-guy—and before you ask, no, I never figured out the director's name. My contact in L.A. said he had it but it was too "valuable," whatever that means. I'm sure once I can get to a decent research library I can pull up some more info and probably find it, but whatever. There's fucking nothing online on it."

FORGETTING

Questions. But what? Nothing, certainly. He is gone now. His spectre haunts everything; every living room, every kitchen, every hallway, every bathroom. Every bed.

Considering the act of love again. Something—nothing. His body was perfect. Channel the perfection into a signifier. No, nothing is signified. Not a sign, just a remnant. He may as well have committed suicide. Don't remember what actually happened. His voice, gone. Never really there to begin with. Presence, no. Echoes. His voice was never more than an echo.

Cannot. Cannot. Cannot. Where is the answer that's sought. He haunts this house. He haunts all houses. Trying to avoid despair. Thrown into desperation.

Compare and contrast: Despair with Desperation, Loss with Death, Hopelessness with Recklessness, Giving-up with Urgency, Absence with Presence, the Possible with the Impossible.

An email from a contact in New York:

Hey—

I vaguely remember reading an interview, in a photocopy of a film-zine, with a man who claims to have attended a "discreet screening of a snuff film." The interview mainly confronts his "extreme" experiences and "what exactly it is that [he's] looking for that has lead [him] down [his] path." His responses are mostly boring: some desire to "confront the reality of death and sexuality," the same old crap that melodramatic serial killers tend to call upon when asked why they killed victim X or victim Y. The man is obviously an idiot.

To dismiss the interview right off the bat would be unwise though, as a few tangential details—regarding the man you are looking for—seem to appear among the "in between" of what he's talking about. My scanner's fucked up right now so I can't just sent you a copy of the article (I don't have the time to just type it up right now), but what I can remember is that, as part of one of the "discreet screenings" he's attended, what sounds like one of your mystery director's short films was played. He describes the night as mostly "bullshit, mind-numbingly dull short films that jaded porn directors with sudden pretensions of grandeur make in order to move away from the desperate lives they've made for themselves" (as if this man doesn't fit the precise description he's accusing others of).

He describes several of the shorts, mostly to humor the interviewer (whose questions are more interesting than the man's answers), and, as I said, one of them sounds like your man. He describes a five minute scene that has a camera wandering down a hallway in what seems like an institutional building, perhaps a commercial warehouse. Doorways line both sides of the path, and as the camera tracks down the hallway a wide-angle lens barely reveals sexual couplings occurring on sterile looking beds in blank white rooms. The camera remains focused on the end of the hallway, and as the presumed goal is finally reached, the camera quickly turns around to reveal all of the men that had formerly been part of the sexual couplings (mostly off camera) standing nude, staring at the lens. After revealing the crowd, the camera quickly pans up to find a man—possibly this Garrior you mention—harnessed in a sling, eyes shut, a look of complete absence on his face.

Of course, the man is laughing as he relays this info, casting off-base judgments and basically ruining any indication of the actual tone of the piece. Sorry this is vague; once I get my scanner fixed I'll send you a copy.

Best of luck,

E--

GHOSTS

The best idea is to circle around the story that you want the film to tell. To let it creep up on the viewer, unexpected. Then let it pop up like an apparition, the result of a séance. Consider Dante's circles of hell, but subvert them. Consider the structure of a circle and what it inherently leads to: to posit the circles within a system of verticality is to delineate the true potential of the autonomous geometry. Circles work best being moved from the inside out, like a Grecian labyrinth found on the back of an antiquated coin: move from the outside-in, with an increase in intensity as you get closer to the center. Then at the center: not nothingness, but a *full sense of absence*; something missing.

That is what human beings are most terrified of; that is the absolute of despair and pain. The only true "presence" of evil in the world is "absence." A hole in the middle.

But to ignore the binary opposition of presence/absence is to ignore the double: the specter, the phantom. The story, like a phantom, can be neither present nor absent; neither live nor dead. This is how narrative works best, especially in considering the pornographic imagination. An obvious ennui becomes banal, unexciting. Repetition in the wrong way. Eroticism is a secret, a mystery. Absence versus presence: neither one can win. Neither can lose.

HAUNTED

Potential narrative:

> A tracking shot circles the outside of the architecture. The building is seven stories tall and isolated in the middle of a destroyed country, the structure perfectly vertically rectangular. As the camera makes its slow and steady trawl around the building, images of a couple fucking violate the screen in increments based on a rhythmic schemata. The images are very subtle at first, hovering within view for no more than two seconds at a time. After several passes around the building, the camera confronts the entrance directly.
>
> As the camera pulls toward the door, the pornographic interruptions occur more frequently until a fairly consistent strobing is developed; the frame alternating between the door and the images of coupling. Once the door is finally opened the pattern stops and the screen is abandoned to an overexposed white (a sense of ALL-OVERNESS pervades).
>
> We are now inside the structure, positioned on the first floor: the camera explores the space in a manner similar to that used in communicating the exterior of the building. Once again a schemata violates the interior in favor of the sex act (a variation of the first). Each shot

lingers twice as long as before, i.e. four seconds instead of two.

A stairway around the inside periphery of the space connects the first floor to the second, the second to the third, etc. On each floor the film's structure is repeated, with the elements of pornography slowly overwhelming the architecture in the film, until on the fourth floor the scenes of the interior are reduced to two second shots that punctuate the sexual activity.

After the seventh floor and seventh sex scene have been fully explored, a low rumbling invades the soundtrack. The camera (no longer punctuated by sexual activity) floats toward a formerly ignored elevator located at the center of the building. Upon entering, the lens of the camera points directly up (the spectator-as-camera is now in the exact middle of the building).

A man—a man who, the spectator realizes, has been a participant in every sex scene, only fully revealed at this point—appears in the elevator as the camera pans back to a horizontal position. We see the elevator doors shut. The camera is in the elevator, and above the man the viewer can see floor numbers light up one after another. The elevator moves slowly. As the elevator, and numbers, descend, the man strips, a look of detachment taking over his face.

Upon arriving back on the first floor, the man, now fully nude, turns to face the elevator doors. They open, and he walks outside. Again, an overexposure of light reduces the image to an unending sea of whiteness. The

> man is gone, but as audience we are forced to question whether or not he was really there, or whether he was only occupying the space of the film.

The answer, of course, is no. He is an image invading another image, a ghost of a desire that permeates a manifestation of desire.

"Anyway; Garrior had apparently made a ton of shorts with the dude before they started filming the feature. But, like, the director was too stuck in the world of art films to be okay with just commercially distributing his work. He tried to enter the work into festivals: this is why I'm sort of assuming that perfect dude was credited as 'Paul Garrior' in these films. You know: ex-porn star trying to make something intellectually valid, it generally leads to a name change. But the shorts were way too fucking out-there for standard experimental festivals in America.

"Apparently a horror festival fond of experimentation & sex in France accepted some of his shorts, and he gained some notoriety. I found some PAL pre-record on eBay that was potentially one of the director's shorts; it's possible, but Garrior is nowhere to be found and the film itself lacks the aesthetic intensity that's, you know, there, in the other scene, so I can't be sure."

"Any credits on that?"

"Production and Direction are credited to 'Roland Marceignac.' Roland Marceignac was a pseudonym that Jess Franco used at some point in his career. I'm pretty sure that the film wasn't a Franco film: Franco rarely dealt with male homosexuality—the few times he did, it was generally as camp or comic relief. Plus Franco didn't really make shorts. Who knows."

INFINITUDE

The narrative that doesn't end. Life? Too obvious, boring. And life does end. Life ends repeatedly, every day. The world? It will end too, eventually. Sooner than later. Aesthetics. Phenomenological; if life and the world end, aesthetics end. What then.

Perhaps death isn't an ending. Straying close to cliché again. On the streets of Paris a hustler once begged, "I want this to last forever." It was ridiculous, but he meant it.

(He never said that though.)

Memory, experience, once again phenomenological. Inherently so. Consider the philosophers' absolute truths. Are they eternal? Eternal is the wrong word. An absolute truth cannot be considered finite. But absolute truths cannot be experienced, and are conceptual to begin with. Ideas. A never ending idea.

Nothing. A void. A black hole.The moment of sexual climax. Ends too soon. Making it last forever is impossible. What is infinite? The impossible.

I had a dream last night:

> I find myself attached to Icarus's wings. I spread them and jump, begin to fly. I consider the history of the wings: I will not fly too close to the sun, for the sun is God and I know God is dead. I have nothing to fear.
>
> With my arms spread to maximum length, it is easier to describe my action as gliding than flying. Below me an infinite void stretches. Turning my head reveals the same absence in all directions. The sun—God, who is dead—is nowhere to be seen. I can see nothing, but I get a distinct feeling that I am actually seeing everything.
>
> As I lust further and further into the void I am ensconced by a feeling of pleasure. I have no worries, no anxieties, the idea of despair seems ridiculous. This void is sublime.
>
> Hours pass and nothing is changing. I have never felt better. Hues shift around me, but they are not colors I could identify on any discernible spectrum. I realize that I am fading into the anti-world around me.
>
> As I become less and less of a material object, the feelings of perfection that have kept me safe for the entirety of my flight begin to dissolve. Anxiety and terror overcome me.

I wake up and discover I have come during sleep.

User reviews from the IMDb entry for *Haunt Me, Haunt Me* – directed by J. Riverrun, 1973.

I've seen Haunt Me Haunt Me 30 years ago, made a great impression on me, 15 August 2006
Author: christian-318 from Lalouret, France

I give 9 out of 10 because I'm not sure the film has stand it through the years. Otherwise, in my memory, it's one my real favorite one. I remember that I was like hypnotized by this movie. It was also this film that made me adore Paul Garrior (he is so great in "Ledermeister" from Colt Films, another cult-movie for me). Some scenes are still alive in my mind. Especially when the whole world "prays" to help the hero fly away through mind-force. It's a SF story but with a very particular mood. Calm, strange, soft, very bright lights. It's one of these movies that I really would like to see again. The story has something in common with "Blow Job" from Alberto Cavallone. This play with time, eternity, things happening softly, with no stress, no running, and so much weirdness. I also remember the music was aerial. I don't know if this movie is existing somewhere, if it can be seen or bought but I'd like to.

Before you get your hopes up.... No, I haven't seen this film :-(, 13 March 2005
Author: DC1977 from United Kingdom

I am itching to see this film.
I remember about 6 or 7 years ago, Al Parker was

interviewed by Mark Cousins on the BBC. This film was mentioned and there were actually clips shown. One showed Garrior hanging out of a window, another walking alongside an active volcano and a third on a beach with water approaching him from all sides. Cousins (who is an absolute movie geek but also a real film expert, unlike Barry Norman) said he has never seen the film nor does he know anyone who has seen it. It appears that some people have seen this film because it has received votes. Although this may be a vote based on what they have heard about the film's quality rather than through having seen it. PLEASE, PLEASE, PLEASE contact me if you know how this film can be obtained. I tried contacting Mark Cousins and even Paul Garrior's old agent to find the whereabouts. I never got a reply from Cousins and unsurprisingly Garrior's agent couldn't help. But I had to try...

JEALOUSY

Erased. Useless, really. But maybe people just tell themselves that. Consider the implications of a viewer and the film-image. Jealously over the perfection found, a distance, a representation. The movies can cover up flaws. Convince the viewer that there are no flaws to begin with. Jealousy as empathy. An active viewing experience: the spectator lusts over the subject of the film.

Should jealousy of Paul affect—sorry. Dishonest to continue that thought. Maybe not.

Where is Paul today. Hasn't called.

Jealously as empathy—that is what is at stake here. A body on the screen. A body the spectator wants.

"You know, I'm surprised you're actually interested in this."

"Why?"

"I don't know. You're prone to ignoring my obsessions."

"This one's different."

"How?"

"Because it's not the same as the others."

"Don't be a smart-ass, just answer the question."

"Well, I don't know. I guess it's just, well, you act like you've come face to face with God in the screen of your television via an antiquated pornographic video tape. I mean, to be fair you always have something new to rave about whenever I see you, but this time it seems different."

"It's been over a year since you've come to visit me."

"I know, I know, and I'm sorry about that. But really—how long have you been after this?"

"What do you mean by 'this'?"

"I mean— this guy—what's his name— Garore."

"Garrior."

"Right, yeah, him. I mean, well, okay: you were, like, completely absent while we were fucking earlier."

"What?"

"I don't know. It's been a while, but before it always seemed like no matter what had happened, no matter how long it had been, you were always super present. I mean, it just seemed different this time. It seemed like, well, you barely moved, and normally you're like really into it, you know?"

"Well, yeah, of course I know. But really? It seemed like I wasn't there?"

"I don't know. I mean, it probably wasn't exactly how I'm describing it—like, I mean, well, I guess what I'm trying to say is that it just didn't seem as urgent, the way sex with

you normally does. But whatever, how long have you been looking for him, so to speak."

"I watched the tape a week or so after you left last time. And that was what, last May? And it's June now, so yeah, a little over a year."

"Have you been this intense about it the whole time?"

"I don't know. I mean, I guess. You know how I get when I'm obsessed with something. Passing time? Plus, I mean, I don't know, this is like exactly what I've been looking for. Like, all of my obsessions my entire life have centered around something that's missing, something terrible. And all of my obsessions have always been concerned with stories, movies, media. It just feels oddly like the perfect summation of my life's 'work,' so to speak. I mean, I guess that sounds kind of stupid, but, you know."

"Yeah, I guess I do."

KINESIS

To make the camera the spectator's eye. When the light is too bright, an eye closes, blinks, squints. What does a camera do, faced with overexposure? Blink the shutter, shatter the image, interrupt. Interrupt—that is the answer. The camera as extension of the eyeball, reacting to an external (though in this case, diegetic) stimulant. When a person sees something vile, they turn away. When a person sees something that fills them with lust, they stare. The camera, like the eye, must penetrate the subject. A slow, subtle, unnoticeable zoom will provide this penetration.

Lexicon of movements for camera-as-eye
Squint: a blurred or vignetted image.
Close, sleep: blank screen, slow fade-in of dream image.
Blink: external interruption (cut), disruption.
Shocked: quick pan away from subject.
Stare: slow zoom.
Headache, pounding in eyes: quiet strobe.
Rubbing eyes until spots appear: the infinity of the universe, stars.
Wink: quick jump-cut zoom.
Cross: colour separation, image displacement.
Twitch: quick, short, loud strobe.
Stoned: every object and subject on screen equally in focus, flat.

Four lobby cards sit in the basement of an abandoned film archive in New York City. The owner used to brag that Amos Vogel attended screenings at the archive (as if Vogel weren't permiscious in his attendance of screenings to begin with). In later years, screenings, and to a lesser extent, the content of the archive itself, were overrun with the disposable pornography required to make a profit.

The lobby cards all share a similar layout. A six inch by nine inch piece of matte card stock, an image printed in the center with a ¼ inch white border. At the top left corner of each (and each layout is positioned horizontally), identical text sits in front of an oblong white circle: "The Abyss is the Foundation of the Possible," and below that, in a smaller font, "J. Rivverrun / P. Garrior." No other identifying marks can be found.

The first image: a nude body collapsed on the ground of an endless hallway. As the hallway fades to a vanishing point, projected light has layered a white grid on top, carefully defining the angles of the space. The muted neutrality of the hallway is violated by harsh primary hues spilling out of doorways that punctuate the space. This man appears in three of the four lobby cards.

The second image: two men on a bed smiling at each other. The most straight-forward image of the group, interrupted only by a thick film grain and slightly distorted presence; as if the image were shot using an extra-wide angled lens barely saved from a fish-eyed level of distortion.

The third image: a group of men in black cloaks standing in a semi-circle, surrounded by abject, neon-colored shapes that float in the air (created by primitive optical tricks, but effective nonetheless). On the floor in front of the men, a nude man (the same as before) lies in the middle of a white diagram (evoking the idea of the pentagram present in black magick rituals, but more obscure) on top of a black floor.

The fourth image: a woman standing in a void, staring at something off camera. She is visible only from shoulders up, and strange lighting casts shadows in the emptiness that surrounds her. This image is the most surprising, and potentially revealing of the group: the film, from all potential resources available, was presumably shot as an all male pornographic film. the woman in the image, at least from what can be seen, appears to be nude.

LIVING

The chambermaid in a 19th century home. The couple exploring the new house they have just bought together. A first apartment. Moving. Discovering a space with someone else, discovering space alone. Making a room a bedroom. Servants kept hidden from the masters of the house. A dinner party held with one's closest friends. A dinner party held with society's elite. We are rich. We are poor. We are somewhere in between.

The atonal drone of existence! Shifting from a higher to lower range. Open the blinds, let some light in. It's dark. Spinning, looking. Explore the contours of everywhere. Waiting for a phone call. Turn a record on. Light candles, the wind will blow them out. A fireplace with ivy on the hearth. This is ridiculous! But it makes one feel something.

Comfort is ridiculous. What does the furniture have to do with living. Potted plants hanging from a skylight. Bodies moving back and forth, around, to and from, where are we going. Sit down. Rest. The bed, existing inside of it. So affected by what is around. People, furniture, walls, high-ceilings, wood floors. The kitchen is dirty!

A dream about packing. I noticed cameras. "Why do you have that?" It is, for me, for everything. It is everything. "I will document the end of it all, right from the start." Someone else is in the room, someone I have never seen before. Stars of the image. Confused for a minute, consider the fact that I am actually awake. Realize I can't be, there are no photographs hung on the walls of this bedroom. Don't remember coming here.

The man tells me his theories regarding sex and I notice we are fucking bareback. But it is okay because this isn't real.

I am talking to someone in a field, a friend. She asks me why there aren't more ghosts around. I tell her, "I assume most people actually, you know, die. I'm pretty sure that I'm still here because I have more to do before finishing dying. The day I died I knew it was going to happen, but I didn't mind so much because I somehow knew that I could stick around."

"You've been quiet for a while."

"Yeah, I don't know. I mean, I've been thinking."

"About what?"

"About you, I guess. Why do you always come back? I mean, I generally understand why you leave: every time that you've done it before it's made perfect sense. But I mean, why always come back to it? To us?"

"Well that's a little melodramatic."

"Yeah, admittedly so. But it's like, I don't know. I mean we both have totally separate lives, and obviously whenever you're here it's always a vacation for both of us. But I'm trying to, like, justify the entire situation. Like, if we conceptualize our relationship as a narrative, where does it climax?"

"Well, I'm pretty sure we both climax pretty regularly."

"Oh come on. I mean, yeah. You're right. Whatever, I'm just over-thinking everything."

"Nah, I'm being a jerk. I don't know. I guess I just know that if I didn't come back every once in a while you'd probably go off the deep end with one of your obsessions."

"I can't tell if you're joking or not."

"Hah, I can't either to be honest. I mean, I don't know. This Garrior obsession is pretty intense."

"But what if, like, this is it. Like, what if this is actually what I've been looking for?"

"What is it you're looking for?"

"Something impossible."

"Everything is possible."

"Then the summit of existence."

"Then I think you might be looking in the wrong places."

MANSION

Potential narrative:

> Abandoned hotel with 28 rooms on 3 successive floors. One of the rooms—the secret 28th room—holds a gateway to hell, a black hole, the concentrated remains of an "Indian burial ground", a dead horse mummified by toxic chemicals (left by a guest affiliated with the occult), an anthropomorphic body devoid of any orifice or eyes, Pandora's box, a monster, parts of an alien spaceship, God, the physical manifestation of terror, absence, a salve that instantly removes all memory of childhood, the sun, or a general void (negative space).
>
> A stranger is taken to this hotel by a local man he meets at a bar several blocks away. The two fuck, and afterwards, while the local sleeps in the neglected room, the visitor wanders the hotel, fascinated by the fact that such a small, empty town once hosted such an elaborate, modern hotel.
>
> Of course, he finds the secret room. He was probably looking for it. He opens the door, which is accessed through another, not-secret room, and comes face to face with whatever is in the hidden space. He suffers one of three reactions: terror, pain, or happiness.

The scenario repeats—the visitor the same man each time, the local different—until all three potential reactions have been reached. After this the hotel explodes, implodes, disappears, becomes invisible, sinks into the ground, catches on fire, floats into the sky, transforms into another building, fills with water, or crumbles to the earth.

Before the destruction of the hotel a medium shot reveals a reflection of the moon visible in every window.

(MURDER)

NOWHERE

All films must not take place anywhere. Location evokes too much. The audience, the spectator, if he or she recognizes a location the diegesis of the film is shattered. The spectator is removed.

A closed set, created on a sound-stage, in a studio: also useless. The level of artifice is interesting, but too limited. It is best to simply make the camera probe the known until it becomes unknown. Perhaps the most important thing learned from Frans: a domestic space can become terrifying. That a camera can defamiliarize the familiar. Obvious, possibly, but Frans did it in such a remarkable manner. Even having been in his house, where he shot most of his shorts, one could not match what was visible on film with what was actually there.

The absence of a recognizable location places the action of a film in a void, leaving more room for images and sound to come together without context. Thus, no pre-existing expectations ruin what has been created. This has all already been said. This has already been established.

It is easiest to be asleep.

Rivverrun did an interview for *Midi-Minuit Fantastique* in 1976. Digging up the volume at the only library in the country carrying the back issues reveals that all but a single page of the interview have been torn out. A translation of that page follows.

So why did you decide to make the move to pornography?
I got tired of stopping myself from trying to get at what it was that I was after. I started making films to communicate something: not the idea of my own self, I've never been a bourgeois, but something that I thought was missing from the world. Pornography, I realized, was the only way to get at that expression. To approach the themes that obsess me—longing, memory, emptiness—one must confront the body honestly. To deal with sexuality without resorting to porno is a lie. It's dishonest. It's hiding the truth. Eroticism without pornography is a lie. But I knew that simple pornography wouldn't get me anywhere near what I was looking to express either. If I had said, simply, "oh, in this film I am going to have two people fucking in this room, and then I will shoot the next scene in this room," that wouldn't have said anything. That would have been just representation. The image has to transcend the idea of representation. Abstraction is what brings out the heart of an idea. So I said to myself, "It doesn't matter that this will not make money. I have never been looking for money. I will make the films that I want to make, the films that have potentiality to attain this idea."

What is the idea that you're after with your films? What are you trying to express?

I'm not sure if I can fully articulate it in words. If I could, there would be no reason for me to make films. It is an idea best not described, because I think it is more of an experience that I want to be able to find whenever the film is watched. It is not just something passive. Film as a medium has many opportunities to interact with its audience in different ways. Beyond the image there is time, there is movement, there is sound. There is the fact that one sits in a dark room, there is the flicker of the light on the screen as the film passes through the projector, there is the atmosphere of the theater. To get closest to what I'm trying to express I think a list of words would suffice, but it would be a very long list, and I feel almost as if the words are sacred, they are sigils. When they are combined, when I put them together, the way that I mean them, into something whole, a film, it is a conjuration of a spirit, and that spirit is what I'm after. It's not something concrete. Perhaps it is best to say that the films I make, all of them, are just the detritus of my search for what I haven't found.

And you're happy with your new film, *The Abyss is the Foundation of the Possible*?

It is not finished yet, but as I work on it, more and more, I feel as if I am getting closer. I can feel a specific energy in every frame of the film, a strange sort of verticality. It is the longest film I have ever considered, and this length I think is something that I should have tried sooner. I feel like I am so close now. Of course, part of why I have become so much more satisfied with my work of late is the relationship with Paul. He is a physical manifestation of what it is that I'm looking for. I found him and never want him to disappear. It is sentimental, perhaps. If I were a simpler person, if life were not something uncomprehendingly complex, instead of making films I would just be satisfied in my relationship with Paul. A normal person would not need anything else. He has helped my work more than anyone else. You can read all the philosophy and poetry you want, but none of that can add up to the experience—the sensuality—of laying your hands on a perfect body. So yes, I am happy with the new film. Very happy.

You've shown me a few pages of the script; it looks more like fractured poetry than a standard scenario. Is this how you normally work?
Yes. As I said before, if words were enough I would not need to make films. In this regard, my scripts are mere ideas compiled together. I use what most refer to as the script simply as an organizing method. The final product rarely bears little relation to my notes. The script is a mere formality: I have to have something to show potential investors, to show actors, sound designers, and so on. My scripts come from notebooks I keep before the genesis of each film. I make a list of words and alphabetically work through them. I hope to one day have enough of a style established that I can rid myself of the script. Working straight from an idea, that is more pure. There is nothing in between the idea and the film. That is how I hope to work in the future.

ONLY

Limits. Structuralist film is interesting, it presupposes that the material qualities of the film are what hold its true ontology: the film in itself. Patterns, a fixed angle, strobing, rephotographing; all of these are important qualities of film that one would be an idiot to ignore. But one is also somewhat of an idiot to ignore everything but these qualities alone. The film is a material, and one must become aware of that material, but if one is aware of nothing but this material, the film will fail. The film does not even have to be watched; one can simply look at the score that the director has used as the film's matrix. Ernie Gehr has approached what is closest to transcending the imposed limitations of structural film: *Serene Velocity* works primarily to affect our persistence of vision—Gehr is tricking the viewer, but this trick is transparent. The spectator is not closing in on the hallway. The spectator is submitting his brain, his eyes, his sense of viewer-becoming to the image.

But that is not all! There is a tone, an atmosphere, a subtle narrative that keeps the viewer becoming! The hallway is dimly lit and abject. To watch the film is to submit to a constant state of terror for its runtime. But would one describe the film as a horror film? Never. One would probably describe the film simply as structural. Ignoring everything outside of what it is that the current artist's system enforces as being 'that which matters.' The symmetry is uncanny. The left side encounters the right side and the double stakes a claim over the eyes of the audience.

Harness this, do not forget it. Gehr has a lesson that should be learned by all. But this lesson is only the beginning. It is terrifying that we, as spectators, will never reach the end of the hallway. Never actually get closer. The hallway doesn't even exist. Space collapsed within, on, the film itself.

Gehr himself was too caught up with the materiality of his project. Notice the lack of music, the lack of sound. To consider such elements of the filmmaking process as 'distractions' from the structural implications of the film is to ignore the potentiality of multiple elements making up a whole. The structural has been examined, let us now take the structural, the material, and add sound, story, and above all, feeling.

"What exactly do you mean by 'the summit of existence?'"

"I don't know. It's probably just some stupid concept I've come up with from reading too much."

"Shut up. It seems like a valid thing to look for, I'm just wondering exactly what it is that you mean. I mean, that's a pretty fucking potent idea."

"I guess so."

"Well?"

"I guess I'm just looking for something that, you know, makes everything worthwhile? I mean, I refuse to accept the idea that everything I've ever cared about, present company excluded of course, is completely useless. Like, I feel like everything before has been leading up to something, and it's something important; it's something that will change the entire-fucking-way that I live my life."

"So basically you're looking for something that makes 'life worth living.'"

"Oh come on, it sounds so banal when you put it that way."

"Whatever, I basically just said what you said except a lot more succinctly."

"Maybe, but it's not just that. It's not just, like, motivation."

"Really. What else then."

"God, I don't know. I mean I guess motivation is part of it. But that's not the whole thing. What I'm looking for is an answer. But not a direct one. I want a map, but I want the locations on the map to not have names. I want an answer in the form of an experience."

"I think you're talking in circles."

"I want material abstraction."

"Well, whatever. Do you want to know what I want?"

"What?"

"I want you on the bed. Now."

PANIC

Extended hysteria. The film: unending suspense without relief. The best way to afflict terror is to create the image of lust, of love, and to violate it, and then to not let go, not let up UNENDING TERROR WITHOUT RELIEF. Senses dull, so the terror, the fear, the suspense, must always be new, different, abstract, abject. Establish the comfortable and violate.

A potential narrative structure:

> A camera crawls through the various floors and stairwells of a house (here, consider modern architecture, particularly that of Brazil).
>
> Landing (of course, this image is becoming stale, but it is just a sketch, it can be refined at a later time) on a couple in bed, two muscular bodies (cannot think outside of Paul) in the grips of each other, inhaling, devouring each other. The bed is the primary object in the room, the men on top of it. A lamp (also modern) sits next to the bed, dimly illuminating the room.
>
> Before penetration has begun, the lights abruptly turn off. We are left with darkness; moaning and panting bodies. The lights come back on, and something is different.

It is subtle, but the minimal furniture in the room has been adjusted. It might not be noticeable, but it is clear that something is different, that something is wrong. Hitchcock's bomb.

The lights go off again, and this time the furniture remains, but one of the men is different. Similar body type, similar face, but someone else. Perhaps a set of twins would be ideal?

Now the camera will pull away from the scene, back into a hallway, until the bedroom, where the coupling is occurring, is in the middle of the frame, taking up, perhaps, only a quarter of the screen. The rest of the house, of the architecture, has turned dark. Shadows exist, but light fails to reach them. The sex becomes wilder and wilder, building until the men are screaming, violently fucking, hitting each other in throes of lust. As this is happening, while the intensity of the fucking rises, dim light begins to reveal terrible markings on the walls of the hallway. Esoteric symbols, something.

Throwing the tilt and swing of the camera distorts the lens: the angles of the hallway become terrible, unreal. Still, beyond the hallway, in the light (which is becoming brighter: whiteness is overtaking the bedroom) the bodies continue to destroy each other sexually. The image has attained a level of confidence, the tone has reached a level of alarm. Something has to happen. The film maintains this state for 2, 3 minutes.

Next the image itself begins to flash. On and off, the sounds of the men ending in climax. Not just once, but every time the image returns. The image has begun to stutter. Image/whiteness/image/whiteness and the end.

Entries from the 1971 *Film-Makers Cooperative Catalogue No. 5:*

> RIVERRUN, Jacques:
>
> IN[T/N]ER//SECTION (1971) 16mm. 12 min. Color. Rental: $8.00
>
> "Structural film dividing the space of a bedroom and that of a hallway into a single 'becoming.' The lengths of shots follow a score based on Rivverrun's recording of how much time he spent in each (bedroom, hallway) during a single week. Near the films' end a man appears, in both the bedroom and the hallway, violating the absence that each spatial archetype has established." —W.D.
>
> METEMPSYCHOSIS (1968) 16mm. 3 min. B&W. Rental: $6.00
>
> "Opening with a shot of a nude body lying static on a bed, what follows is a quick-cut series of landscapes and nature abstracted by a wide-angle lens. A careful rhythm develops as a slight narrative progresses us from the body to the never ending sky, here depicted by an excess of light, where a face is carefully superimposed in the blinding white." —W.D.

QUESTIONS

1. What do you expect when you watch a film?

2. How involved in a film do you generally find yourself?

3. Would your interest in film change if the act of watching a film required more work?

4. Have you ever seen an image you have never forgotten? If so, describe the image.

5. Do you regularly watch films under the influence of drugs or alcohol? If so, how does this affect your viewing of the film?

6. Do you regularly have nightmares?

7. Do you consider pornography a legitimate art form?

8. Do you consider yourself relationship-compatible?

9. What influences your decision to see a film?

10. Have you ever lost someone violently close to you?

"When you leave this time you're not coming back, are you."

"What?"

"Come on. I mean, I can just tell."

"I don't know."

"Well, okay. I never know when or if you're coming back anyway, so I guess this won't make a huge difference."

"I wanna see it."

"See what?"

"The film. Or, the segment. Whatever it is you've tracked down."

"Are you, I mean, are you sure? I thought that the whole sex & death thing kinda freaks you out."

"Come on. Show it to me."

RITUAL

CLEAR THE BED OF THE FIRE OF LOVE

Banishment of jealousy // banishment of placidity

Acephale: What thou wilt is not what thou want.

Tonal repetition 5-5-5-5-5
Priest strikes light upon ground, 3-3-3, 5-5-5-5-5, 3-3-3
Fade tone and dim lights upon altar.

Acephale: Let all adore the Body of Man

All do the god form of
MANY, the lust of
ALL, facing Altar.

NONE
Acephale picks up light and strobes toward the East, standing in the West.
(Emptiness, explode with)
ALLAHIJEN DAMMATON TZILLIBET (all repeat)
F'NIGH (all repeat)

BITTER (all repeat)
Acephale: In the sacred words and angles:
GOD * NONE * ENODH *

In thy self: RESIST

Acephale: I declare the sacred light one and eternal in all worlds seen and unseen.
(priest raises strobes)
Acephale: Glory be the light, forever trapping the escaping darkness. Forward, until.
(all repeat)
Priest raises intensity of strobes in bedroom.
Acephale: Hail those from the caverns of the dark, the bodies of the gods.
(sign of absent-lust)
Tone: 3-3-3 5-5-5-5-5 3-3-3
(sign of silence)

Acephale: O great and dreaded God of Shadows
He who is destroyer of all Life & giver of Lust,
It is Thee we invoke. (all repeat last line)

Acephale: Behold, the West is Ameti, Land of the Dead to which our body hath gone for rest and release.

OPEN WIDE THE GATES THROUGH WHICH ALL MUST PASS
ALLOW THE ANGLES AN EQUILIBRIUM IN SPACE
LET THE SHELLS OF THE ABSENT BODIES RETURN TO OUR NIGHTS

GUIDED BY THE SACRED STROBE SEEN IN ALL WORLDS
CLIMB UPON US, ALL ARE TRULY WELCOME TO OUR BODY.
MAY YOU REMAIN AMONG OUR SWEAT AND BILE TILL THE FIRST LIGHT OF DAWN...
IN TERROR AND CHAOS
APPROACH THE BODY OF OUR CASTLE (all repeat)

3-3-3, 5-5-5-5-5, 3-3-3
(intensity of strobes increase)

Acephale: Hail those from the labyrinths of the dark body.
(all repeat)

pick up contract at sacrifice;

EMPTY BODIES HERE THIS NIGHT, TO YOU WE GIVE OUR SACRIFICE
UPON THIS PAPER WE HAVE EJACULATED A CONTRACT BINDING OUR LUST TO SOULS
SO INTO THE FLAME OF NIGHT & LET IT BE DESTROYED
IT IS FOR YOU AND I, NO ONE ELSE.

as written, to bind the contract, drink of the body.

...done

So mote it be (all repeat).

After all have sacrificed seed; all raise hands upward, vibrating NONE

Acephale: Our spilling done, I proclaim this evening rite over.

THE BODY IS HEADLESS, TO SACRIFICE IS WILL. (all repeat)

(REALITY)

Polled by Sight & Sound magazine, Catherine Breillet included Riverrun's feature film on her top ten. Whether or not she had seen the entire film at the time is unknown. Her list also includes Pasolini's *Salo*, Lynch's *Lost Highway*, and Kazan's *Baby Doll*, among other admittedly-conservative choices. About *The Abyss Is the Foundation of the Possible* she has to say:

"First, because I wouldn't otherwise have been able to make *Romance*. It made me understand that an image is not pornographic in itself, it's the way we look at it that renders it pornographic. More generally, I'd say that the image doesn't exist in itself, but is deciphered through our emotions. It is the means through which film-makers translate their ideas. This is why I make personal films, because in the end it's my signature on the film, even though others contribute to its making"

SILENCE

The silent film is a function of history: before it was possible to cheaply sync sound to a film, it didn't happen. It's not impossible any more—why are so many experimental filmmakers not concerning themselves with sound? One could revert to ideas of materialism, but that doesn't seem enough. Sound is important in cinema. It is another step towards the process of making cinema "complete."

Sound is important. And it is in this regard that silence is important. Silence without context is useless; it is nothing.

(SCREAM)

TOTALITY

Another dream:

> The incident begins with a viewing of a film, and this action is maintained until my perspective switches to that of a first person narrative (i.e. *I am the star of the film*), while I am allowed to observe the events (observe myself) as a spectator. I am simultaneously watching and participating; I exist in two separate layers of diegesis: the diegetic world of the film (as an active spectator), and my unique perspective as Paul's 'love-slave,' the character in the film I am watching, no longer a character but a person with a unique identity situation action and persona.
>
> There is a line of cars in front of a building. One car moves back and forth in front of the other as Paul stands in the foreground, staring at something offscreen. Narration, in a voice of concern, describes an incident involving Paul sodomizing someone, the cars in the background serving as an abstracted visual metaphor. (There is, of course, a disjunct between the 'real world' and the 'film world' here; each seeps into the other).
>
> I am at a supermarket, and something happens. I am forced into a position of guilt and frustration. My groceries, sitting on the edge of a checkout counter, begin to fall to the ground. I feel shame and begin to

clean them up, though the action does not seem to be my fault. As I clean the spilled food and drink (a gallon of milk, a bottle of ketchup; blood red on semen white mixing on the ground in front of me), I see a man and Paul, shirtless, wrestling and groping one another at the wall. As I watch this event I realize that not only am I the man groping Paul, but I am also Paul himself, while another man is me. My position in the narrative constantly slips throughout the entire incident as I watch, take on both roles, and exist as the other at the same time. The two men (me & the other, the other & Paul, Paul & me) sniff each other's arm pits. As a viewer and a participant I am increasingly turned on.

As the men continue their erotic event a "cut" in the narrative leads to me experiencing & viewing a montage of sadomasochistic scenes, all featuring the same men (once again, myself and the other—and it is here that I realize the duplicity of the characters: I am the bottom with Paul, but as a spectator I see that Paul is the bottom—the 'me' that is watching the film comments upon this and becomes more aroused). Another voice-over (the same voice as before), in the form of a news report, comments upon a missing boy who is considered tangential to a girl who has been missing for some time. A cut reveals a scene (that I am no longer participating in, only viewing) in which a nude woman, body contorted into the vague shape of a 'purse,' is left by the side of a road. As the role of the purse, the girl shits in the mud: she is referred to as purse-woman. Paul, or the Other, recites a monologue on the abstracted nature of sadomasochism: during the monologue I am both tied up to a cross-beam and viewing a visual montage of bizarre and out of focus animation that I understand to be allegory of an abstracted SM ideology: a 'life-size' birthday cake stage, pure darkness, colors shifting through a distinct tonal arrangement, an array of toys and models, and more mimetic SM scenes, repressed from the outside world.

Inter-cut with the footage of the abstract montage, a woman (perhaps the purse-woman, perhaps not) runs through a forest. She falls upon the muddy ground (it is raining) repeatedly, but each time gets up and continues to run. Myself as spectator (or the camera) sees her only from behind. The camera (or myself as spectator) does not follow the woman, but remains still and moves from location to location via a series of quick cuts. My spectator-self is reminded of both Alberto Cavallone and Alain Robbe-Grillet. My character-film-world-self is currently absent, but I know that my SM play with Paul continues. I feel myself dissolve as the foot of the film runs through the projector and white light pulls the screen into oblivion.

"Well?"
"What?"
"Say something."
"I can't right now."

"Please, anything."

UNDERNEATH

The surface. The ground. Buried, hidden, obscured. Subtext versus context. The hypnotic image, subliminal. The secrets buried in a tomb. A man's dying wish, taken with him to the grave.

Intentionally gone or accidentally missing.

At a bar downtown there is a subterranean level of which most patrons are unaware. Following a set of stairs in the back, one descends as Orpheus to the underworld, though circumstance dictates that no one is going to be saved. Eurydice will not be tailing back to the land of the living.

The stairs lead to a hallway, adorned with rooms, each room patterned with a window. These are small windows, a square foot in size, and if one's pleasures are limited to those of the voyeur there is much to experience. If one's pleasures expand to a far more active level of participation, there is also much to be found by simply turning a door knob. (What can be seen is not to be described by those attending, yet there is much talk by the clued-in few.) Mere SM fails to articulate the variety found.

One room dedicated to urine, another to shit. One to vomit. A peculiar ventilation system keeps the smell from the bar above, contained for the dedicated few to worship in the cement room. No health precautions are taken at any level. Filth is welcomed by filth: the golden tears of heaven cry upon the cold floor, heating the body before succumbing to the emptiness.

The body, streaked in shades of brown, black, and green, welcomed as defense from the outside world; the body protecting the body. A pile of projected color, hues spanning the absent-spectrum, a storm of bile reigning from above.

The next room a temple of blood, the following room holding ropes and binding material. The next room filled with water, the following room filled with only air, the last room filled with crystal. Another room filled with glass. A room filled with rolls of receipts. A room filled with balloons, a room filled with light. A room filled with nothing. A room filled with expectations.

One expectation is that sexual satisfaction, in one of the rooms below the bar, is possible.

Memory betrays if this is fiction or not.

Pierre Cardinaux attended a lecture on film given by Gilles Deleuze about Jose Benazeraf & Jacques Riverrun at the Sorbonne in the early 80s. He has been gracious enough to transcribe these notes for our project:

> The plot is unimportant:
> rather, what is important is the "epistemic dimension of film" and how the film can relate to the audience, how the audience engages with the film. The internal movement of both Benazeraf & Riverrun's films is occasionally motionless—it is nomadic, stopping for rest, "camping for a very long time." These films are moving without being in motion.
>
> Without offering a guide to translate the movements, the films force the spectator to draw upon "the temporal modalities of her own world," being "what she experiences, imagines herself to experience, what she would experience if she were the character (if there is a character), etc." i.e. an active experience: collecting the actual and the virtual, a "cinematographic network." Distinction from an "entirely virtual" internal language.

VIOLATE

The audience with the film. The film with the body. The body with the camera. There are levels of interaction when we consider a non-passive audience. Gidal insists that the only way to force the audience into a realm of participatory action with film is to rely on the material/structural aspects, to abandon narrative. This is wrong.

A body can charge another body. The spectator can penetrate the film-body. The film-body as the active-body. Surpassing representation, the body becomes not a signifier, but a presence.

The idea of the spectator alone in the dark.

The idea of ignoring the spectator's expectations, moving through the dark without a suspension of disbelief; rather, an active engagement.

Repetition, repetition.

There is no reason to remember anything. Eternal presence, becoming-presence. Light in front of the eyes. A body jumping up: in front of the screen or within the screen? Both. Where are you going (as a spectator, as a film-body, as a creator-body DEATH OF THE AUTHOR). There is no past or future with film, there is only an eternal presence.

No recurrence.

A spectator alone with the light (the film–body, the material-film, the material-body).

(VIDEO)

"I think I sort of understand. I mean, probably not with the same intensity that you do. But I understand where the urgency comes from. There's something there. Something's happening inside of the image."

"Everything is happening inside of the image."

"The sound too... it's really, uh, intense? I mean—It's like quiet and loud at the same time. It kind of fucked me up."

"I know! Isn't it incredible!?"

"Yeah, actually. Incredible is a good word for it."

"Definitely."

"But I have a question: How does sex compare, or like, you know, reality, afterward. After you experience the image, when you're so deeply indebted to it."

"I don't know. I mean, I guess it's something totally separate, like, I don't consider sex and any construction of this perfected fantasy idol to be something on the same metaphorical 'page.'"

"But isn't the lust there either way?"

"Yes, but it's a different kind of lust. My lust, for this film, this dude, whatever, it's endless. It's inside of the image. It's not temporary, it's permanent. It's not real, it's an image. It's like my lust is a representation of my own actual lust, but I can dump that into this image, this tape, and they never have to separate. It's formless. I can't achieve any physical gratification from it, so I have to departmentalize, keep it away."

"But you're so tied to it. How do you justify the absent lust with your day to day life?"

"I think maybe that's what I'm trying to get closer to. A closure in the divide. Some sort of abstract level of experience where the experience within the image is the physical experience."

WIND

A composition of atmosphere:

> The movement of air ruffles sheets on a bed. (Immediate tangent: the photographic erotica of David Hamilton; sometimes boring, sometimes trite, always evocative of a different plane of existence). Light is dim, it is perhaps early morning, perhaps dusk. Perhaps we are inside of a room without any external light and the glow of appliances is all that permits vision. Perhaps noise, perhaps a tonal composition, on the soundtrack. The spectator can feel a heavy fog, but there is nothing on the screen: how? Layers upon layers of the same image, a murkiness penetrating the depth of the image. Buried within the frame is a representation of heavy fog, moving in darkness. This is a trick.

An indication of atmosphere:

> The moon's reflection from the sea on a stoic face, silence. Eyes are shut: as spectators we cannot identify the face in any sort of discernible, realistic location. A heavy-browed head floating in endless darkness, but really it's just a room. The sea ripples through the window, forcing the shadows to vibrate upon the face. Eyes open.

THE ABYSS IS THE FOUNDATION OF THE POSSIBLE
(JACQUES RIVERRUN, 1977)

Long thought lost by cult film aficionados everywhere, Riverrun's only (completed) feature film has finally surfaced. Riverrun was a cult director who, after studying experimental film under Frans Zwartjes at the Dutch Film Academy, moved to the US and began making experimental porno films. His US career began with a few shorts that gained him minor celebrity status at underground and European film festivals, as well as resulting in his films shown in small, generally independently owned repertory houses across the United States. Like all great art, particularly when it comes to film, he never received much acclaim in his day—the closest thing to notoriety he got was a mention, next to Jose Benazeraf, in a lecture that Gilles Deleuze delivered on film.

The Abyss... was recently found when porn-historian Gregory Martin was rooting through some discarded film canisters outside of the last remaining adult theater in North America— the Fox Theater in Vancouver, Canada. Recently under new ownership, it can be assumed that the canisters that Martin found in the dumpster had been overlooked by the theater's former owners upon moving out. Or perhaps they were lost in the labyrinthine hallways of the theater, found only when a wall was knocked down for remodeling. However it happened, film fans truly have Martin to thank for this astounding discovery.

The film as it exists now clocks in at around 13860 feet: about 154 minutes. And even with this seemingly-extensive runtime, there appear to be sloppy splices present, indicating that even more of the film is missing (though with the narrative on display here, it seems like it'd be hard to notice—but more on that later). Shot primarily in color on 16mm reversal stock and blown up to 35mm (at least, according to various records of Riverrun's found by other film historians across the country), the film is truly unique.

The first thing one notices during the duration of the film is that there is a complete absence of dialog aside from two or three lines that are quickly overcome by remarkable sound design (as a note: I would love to find out who was responsible for the sound design in this film, it recalls yet predates the sound design of Philippe Grandrieux's films in terms of intensity). The narrative (which, if you've seen any other of Riverrun's films that have leaked to the public, you probably would have guessed, is entirely abstract) moves through images and sounds, creating a veritable labyrinth of sensuality. In the same way I have insisted David Lynch's *Inland Empire* works as an experiential film, Riverrun's film accomplishes this perfectly (and I'm being sincere here; despite the fact that my reviews are occasionally littered with hyperbole, this I truly, deeply mean).

Colors seem to play an important part, and seem also to work to affect the viewer with tonality in a way that is obviously derived from psychological color associations, but taken to a much deeper level. Light is tricky; some scenes are shot remarkably under-exposed, while others are over-exposed, yet we always get the impression that the image is still present. And as an audience we move through these images, Riverrun's camera working in way that I don't think I can even describe, as language can't express movement in any way that is natural.

While this review might be, admittedly, vague, one must accept the fact that this film is, if anything, *important*. It has completely changed the way I think about cinema, and hopefully it's recent unearthing will infect a new generation of filmmakers with the motivation to work in this manner.

XXX

Two bodies undress, climb into bed. There is a quickness to the act, something imminent. A quickness that acts so no one can tell whether the lights are on or off. Perhaps the eyes are closed, lively lips locked to one another, a sloppiness that betrays the act of love for the lust at the core. With eyes open one can tell that the lights are off and question whether this is the best decision: to see or to feel the act See with the fingers, perhaps they could say, see with the movement of two bodies intertwined into a single mass moving through time. But time has stopped and everything looks choreographed from the inside.

With clothes off shapes take on new forms and movements become shadows of themselves. The darkness remains. Eyes open or shut: there is nothing to see, only sweat to the touch, a biting scent of an endless black hole. One tongue penetrates that hole (provided options: mouth ear asshole). All appendages work their way into a mouth with purpose: a sloshing sucking seriousness haunts the warm air. Perhaps there is panting now, permeating the proud bodies that refuse to give up on one another. Hands are jealous of the forms taken within, doorknobs to the inevitable.

There might be dialogue but mostly only muffled sighs. A quiet and selfless desperation. The sex act has overcome now, dilated members reach beyond their grasp for the other. Questions set forth before the bedroom are abandoned to the frozen, never-ending moment. Keep your eyes shut, pretend that the distance between two people is a myth.

A quick turn finds one on top of the other, one underneath, new positions exploded into uncanny representations of potential non-euclidean spaces. This could never be represented by an image, it can happen only in the deathly silent and absent void of this precise moment. One enters the other, one howls both howl which is not important (for it is both, together). The silence violated by simple noises, movement never stops.

A change finds new shapes, the other on top of the one, a new insertion. Oiled with pure desire, nothing can destroy one as extension of the other. Lust prevents a tearing, one slides into the other with ease, and in the frozen time both know that nothing ever ends, never has to, that the moment lasts for an eternity in comparison to everything else. Neither understands the other at this moment, yet both are concerned with nothing but that which is happening. It could be said that fucking lasts for hours but really in the depth of the act time is fucked to the point of being completely absent from this new world.

"I don't know how to respond to that."
"I don't think you need to."

YEARN

The film must act as the infinitive of the verb. It is impossible to articulate how much I want this, him, nothing.

ZERO

But I know that any film will amount to nothing, and as soon as it's done I will have to begin another. But now, with him gone, I think I must stop.

Selected Film Reviews, 2007-2018

THE BEDROOM
(HISAYASU SATO, 1992)

Hisayasu Sato's *The Bedroom* opens with a surveillance camera being sprayed with black spray paint. Shortly after, the camera shakily pans along the body of a woman, wrapped completely in plastic.

Cut to the apartment of Kyoko and her husband, Esaka, where Kyoko is videotaping her surroundings. "You're bringing out the DEVIO again, then?" Her husband asks. "Yes, It's the only video diary that documents just me and you. Just me and you."

After some semi-flirtatious comments (ignored by her husband), Kyoko brings up the death of someone she knew, a woman who presumably overdosed on a drug known as HALCION. This comment serves as an introduction to much of the narrative that will guide the audience through an exploration of loneliness.

After being repeatedly ignored and rejected by her husband, Kyoko goes to a sex-club referred to as "The Sleeping Room." At The Sleeping Room men act out fetishistic fantasies on unconscious women, essentially doped up on the aforementioned drug Halcion. After a while, Kyoko stops taking the Halcion pills that she is presumably required to take, but still pretends to be unconscious in order to experience the events that take place in the club instead of remaining oblivious to them. Potentially.

Throughout the film, Kyoko's visits to the sex club are generally preceded by Kyoko opening her refrigerator and visually entering a sort of fugue state, but as the film progresses evidence suggests that Kyoko is indeed going to The Sleeping Room.

After one session at the club, Kyoko and another woman discover a corpse--another overdose, echoing the story Kyoko told her husband earlier. Later, Kyoko discovers one of her lover's video diaries. It is Maya, revealed as Kyoko's sister, who was the first victim in The Sleeping Room. Was her lover, Kai, the murderer? Or do the deaths have something to do with Mr. Takano, the enigmatic man who watches over The Sleeping Room through closed-circuit security footage?

The Bedroom works best when considered as a study of depersonalization and loneliness. Throughout the entire film, Kyoko is essentially trying to "connect" with someone. She virtually idolizes her lover, she follows the school girl in order to try to discover "what kind of girls go to The Sleeping Room," and she even avoids taking her pills while in The Sleeping Room in order to experience, connect, with what is going on. Sato further pushes the idea of separation by repeatedly using a distancing effect achieved by moderating the image via video camera, whether to elaborate the disconnect between a character and the situation the character is in, or to emphasize Kyoko's paranoia, at odds with the lonely desperation she normally exhibits. Despite the fact that she seems to be reaching for a connection with anybody, she views the cameras that are watching her as a threat.

Jack Hunter, in an article on Hisayasu Sato, comments that the director's body of work is "dedicated to exposing the dark void at the heart of contemporary existence." *The Bedroom* perfectly illustrates this. With this being said, it would be in bad-faith to discuss the film itself without noting its inclusion of Issei Sagawa as the actor playing the enigmatic Mr. Takano. Issei Sagawa is a Japanese man who, while studying in France, killed and cannibalized a woman in 1981. He was declared legally insane and deported back to Japan, where he spent 15 months in a mental institution and then was more or less able to check himself out. He went on to become somewhat of a fringe celebrity. Sato's choice to include Sagawa is a bold move, and considering the nature of Sato's filmography in its relationship between the mediation of the image and reality itself, also demonstrates that Sato is doing more than trying to use a base means to shock. While the incorporation of an actual murderer into a film about murder itself creates an unnerving mood if the viewer is aware-- the film works just as well if the viewer is not aware of Sagawa's history.

Hisayasu Sato's *The Bedroom* is a bold film which successfully delivers an exploration of depersonalization and loneliness, while still telling an engaging genre story. The visuals are also noteworthy; blue and red light coats the bodies of the comatose girls of The Sleeping Room while giant TVs tuned to constant static decorate the club's walls. Sato's spare use of music also helps to create tension in the film; the soundtrack regularly delivers a tonal buildup that never actually coalesces into climax, keeping the viewer aurally on edge. Despite the fact that the film may seem confusing at first, if the viewer is willing to actively watch the film and engage with the way Sato is telling his story, the viewer is rewarded at the end.

January 3, 2007

DER TODESKING (JORG BUTTGEREIT, 1989)

"This is the King of Death. He makes people not want to live anymore."

Der Todesking was Buttgereit's second film, made shortly after his infamous *Nekromantik*. Buttgereit, to date, only has four feature films to his name; this one, the already mentioned *Nekromantik*, *Nekromantik 2*, and the serial killer film *Schramm*. Due to the reputation he developed via the sensational theme of *Nekromantik* and its sequel, Buttgereit is unfortunately most often associated with plotless gore film and early 90s German splatter flicks. If the viewer expects something hilariously irreverent with *Der Todesking*, they will undoubtedly be let down.

The film's organizing structure is the days of the week, presenting a different suicide daily. On Monday, a man quits his job, writes some letters, feeds his fish, and then overdoses on pills in his bathtub. On Tuesday, a man hangs himself while watching a splatter video. On Wednesday, a woman walks to a park bench in the rain, listens to a man talk about problems with his wife, and then points a gun at him. The man then takes the gun from her, cocks it, and shoots himself in the head. On Thursday, a bridge is shown while names and ages of many people are listed. On Friday, a lonely woman gets a letter in the mail demanding her to take her life after she spies on one of her neighbors. She throws the letter away and eats chocolate, eventually falling asleep. She gazes longingly out her window one more time, and the audience sees the couple she was spying on from her window earlier, dead in their bed. On Saturday, a woman reads somewhat of a manifesto on random mass killings as a form of suicide, then video tapes herself going to a concert and randomly shooting individuals until she herself is shot, and killed. And on Sunday, a man screams and bangs his head against a wall until he slumps to the floor, dead.

In between each day, a body framed in a dark room decomposes. A girl sketches the death king in her notebook. But what does it add up to? If you're willing to give yourself over to the films' unique operating structure, the totality succeeds in adding up to a harrowing image of the self-destructiveness of humanity. The film has no central characters, with each day of the week disconnected from the former, other than in its categorical continuation of the act of self-destruction. What makes the film work is the way that Buttgereit handles the material, and the subtle touches that he throws in at the most unexpected moments. In other words, this is to say that what makes the film work is that Buttgereit actually treats the material with a level of gravitas.

On Monday, the day that launches the film, Buttgereit uses very fluid, creative camera movements to emphasize the small space and banality of the suicide's current existence. On Tuesday, Buttgereit complicates viewer perception by embedding a movie within a movie, within the movie, to heighten the isolated nature of these sad and lonely individuals. Within one of the films-within-a-film Buttgereit has a character frame the blood splatter that's on the wall, creating a casual presentation of violence as art, confronting audience expectations. On Wednesday, Buttgereit actually distorts the image itself, having it loop and stutter in the way decaying video tape tends to do, materially echoing the collapsing mental state of the man in utter desperation. A key to understanding the film is encoded within a letter that the spinster of the Friday episode receives. It begins with a quote from Lautreamont, "We lose our life with joy," and continues to function almost as a Suicide Manifesto.

The film isn't perfect, in itself, as while many of the episodes feel accomplished, others don't work as well. Despite its shortcomings, the film does succeed fully on the level of tone, a pure meditation on death. The film's hauntingly simple score plays a major role in developing the atmosphere and nihilistic mood of the entire film. And it is this tone that leads to the film being worthy of attention and a successful testament to the death drive.

January 14, 2007

THE FRUITS OF PASSION (SHUJI TERAYAMA, 1981)

Shuji Terayama adapted his 1981 film, *The Fruits of Passion*, from the eponymous Pauline Reage's sequel to her well regarded book, *Story of O*. However, 'adapted' is used very loosely in this instance. Terayama uses the opportunity to completely reshape the structure of the novel, and use only its themes and characters to create a story that is uniquely his. According to the credits, the text of the narration and O's dialogue itself was taken directly from the short novel, but everything else is pure Terayama.

At the end of *Story of O* (in both the book and Just Jaeckin's film adaptation), O has surrendered herself completely to Sir Stephen. This film (and the source book itself), picks up directly where that story ends: O is under complete control, and completely in love with, Sir Stephen (in this film, played by Klaus Kinski). Having left France, the two are now in China sometime during the first half of the 20th century. Sir Stephen takes O to a well-regarded brothel run by Madame (played brilliantly by Peter, primarily known for playing transvestite roles throughout his career), where she will be forced to surrender herself to any customers that desire her. O, being blindly in love with Sir Stephen, and willing to go to the extremes of submission, accepts this.

Once the film's motivating narrative has been introduced, Terayama uses a series of brief vignettes to introduce some of the other women at the brothel. There is Aisen, who is convinced that she is a movie star, and who will only screw her customers if there is a camera in the room. There is also Sakuya, a woman who constantly has a peculiar cough, but rarely does anything about it. Other inhabitants of the brothel include dreamers, midgets, overweight women, and the aforementioned, remarkably enthusiastic Madame.

While O is in the brothel, pining for her lover, Sir Stephen is living with Nathalie, a woman who has no comprehension of O and Sir Stephen's relationship, constantly wanting Sir Stephen to give up the relationship, all the while carping on the relationship itself. Eventually, Sir Stephen forces O to watch him and Nathalie make love, but this just proves to O his dedication, as the entire time the two are having sex, Sir Stephen's eyes are fixated on her.

Meanwhile, a young Chinese boy who lives across from the Brothel has fallen in love with O. He joins a group of revolutionaries in order to make enough money to buy O's love. In a subplot that runs throughout the movie (and ties in significantly at the end), attacks are made and eventually the boy is injured. The revolutionary group has some deal made (the specifics are not quite clear, as the dialogue spoken in English is often very hard to understand) with Sir Stephen to finance their weapons for the attack. However, Sir Stephen decides to no longer support their cause, which angers the group, causing them to hold a gun to Sir Stephan's head while the group members steal valuable items from Sir Stephen's house.

Nathalie sees this incident, which causes her to leave Sir Stephen, not wanting anything to do with what she calls a "despicable" man. The same night of Nathalie's departure, the young boy who is in love with O finally gets his money. He buys a new suit and finally enters the brothel. Sir Stephen watches the encounter through slits in the wall.

At first O utterly rejects the boy, caught up with her love of Sir Stephen. She pushes him off the bed when he tries to kiss her, and he falls, landing on the arm he had injured during one of the attacks. Realizing that the boy has suffered much for his love of O, O turns tender towards him, and they kiss, eventually making love.

Sir Stephen, watching this, is devastated when he sees the tenderness that O shows towards the child. O had not been willing to kiss any of her clients before, and this proves a remarkable change. While Sir Stephen has lost himself to myopic affairs, O's submissive tendencies have weakened and she is capable of loving another.

Angered beyond belief, Sir Stephen follows the boy through a sort of casino, where he eventually kills the boy, and then attempts to kill himself. Later, at a sort of social event for the brothel, the character of Death walks up to O, tells her the events that have transpired, and gives the contract that O has signed with Sir Stephen back to her. O is, for the first time in many years, completely free. She has the choice to go where she wants, or stay right where she is.

Viewers expecting the same sort of narrative telling found in *The Story of O*, or even viewers hungry for Jaeckin's soft-focus flavor of eroticism will be sorely disappointed in this film, as Terayama's idiosyncratic aesthetics elevate the story to a level beyond what is found in anything else bearing the Story of O title. Even purely at the level of story, Terayama improves greatly upon his source material: while *The Story of O* is a masterpiece of literature, erotic or otherwise. *Return to the Chateau: The Story of O II* often feels like a lackluster imitation of the book it's responding to.

Terayama fills the film with many of his trademark narrative devices: there is reference to an absent or unremarkable father several times (O's memories, the Chinese boy's father), delirious fantasy that simply echoes the emotional states of the narrative (a grand piano rises from the depths of a river, a woman riding through a hallway on a fake plastic horse), and brilliantly achieved moods resulting from color filters covering the camera lens. Terayama's virtue as a primarily visual director is in full force here, his constant attention to detail notable throughout the film.

J.A. Seazer's music, while departing from the garage-psyche sound of his music for Terayama's earlier films (most notably Throw Away Your Books, Let's Go Out In the Street), is a haunting hybrid of deep bass, synthesizers, and typical soundtrack music, perfectly accenting Terayama's visuals. Beyond the purely plastic elements of the film, Terayama quietly uses a muted psychology to heighten the emotional state of the characters in the film so subtly, that by the time the ending hits, it feels heavier than it otherwise might have.

Something it might be important to point out, however, is how some plot details rely on a former knowledge (or at least familiarity) with the plot of *The Story of O*. The former film explains O's utter submission, and the contract, and knowing what has happened to O before adds to the emotional intensity. It's also worth pointing out that the sex scene looks unsimulated and borders on hardcore, odd for a Japanese production (but I suppose since it was shot mostly in China, that's how it got through the legal system).

While often considered as a minor work in Terayama's oeuvre, and generally derided by fans of the original film adaptation form Jaeckin, *The Fruits of Passion* stands on its own as a brilliant film. Terayama seems to have progressed beyond the hang-ups of his previous feature film, Pastoral: To Die in the Country, where his own biography dominates the narrative. This film is built primarily on the strength of its images, and Terayama doesn't disappoint.

January 22, 2007

SURVEY MAP OF A PARADISE LOST (HISAYASU SATO, 1988)

Hisayasu Sato's brilliant *Survey Map of a Paradise Lost* is a truly singular film. It approaches many of the themes that run rampant through Sato's work of the time (man's relationship with technology, alienation, emptiness, and sexual disorder) using methods that depart from anything that I've seen committed to celluloid.

Nukada is a journalist working on a story about "The Banana Club," a telephone-based BBS sex club. Nukada's coworker Koto knows a girl named Midori who works for the club and offers to set up an interview. Nukada meets Koto for the interview, but before they being, a man pulls up in a car, declares that he had an appointment with Midori first, pulls her into the car, and drives off.

The man is Kihara, a twenty-nine-year-old who works at NDT, a large phone company. He is explicitly interested in Midori, using his position at NDT to insure he is connected to her through The Banana Club. The sex he has with Midori (and for that fact, his wife) is very rough. He has a propensity to tie up his partner and often blood-play is involved.

After a rather strenuous sex session, Kihara and Midori go for a walk, ending up on top of a tall building. Midori tells a story about a pop star who killed herself by throwing herself off a building. She saw this incident occur while she was working in a deli. She remarks how she wants to fall, someday.

The next time Kihara and Midori have sex, the play gets rough and Kihara ends up dead. The incident shows up in the news, and Midori is released of guilt as the video tape ostensibly depicts an act of self-defense. Nukada, aware of the incident, is thrilled when his coworker (the same one who introduced him to Midori) tells him about the existence of the video tape, and then manages to get him a copy. While watching the video tape he notices a few frames of video at the beginning that are not from the night in the love hotel. After freezing the frames Nukada discovers that it is Midori and Kihara's wife talking on top of a roof.

From this point on the film's final act plays out as a series of revelations, allowing the film's tight construction to unravel a sense of narrative shock and desperation. Sato once again proves he is a master of the subversive, using explicit and violent sex to emphasize his themes. Sato also handles his recurring fascination of modern societies depersonalized dependence upon technology greatly, with key elements and scenes playing out on TVs and monitors, slowly being followed by a pan to the actual action; the doubling asks us, as viewers to a) think about our reality versus the reality of the film and b) create a divide in the diegetic motivations and actions of the characters. In a brilliant move by Sato, the ultimate reality of the characters, at the end of the film, is revealed only through the mediated environment of a video cassette.

All said, *Survey Map of a Paradise Lost* is an exemplary demonstration of Sato's narrative power. Its social commentary and artistic achievements (Sato's worldview has always been ahead of its time) are vast. If one can realize that depictions of sadomasochistic sex can serve an ideology as much as it can serve as exploitive titillation, then one can't help but be awed by one of Sato's defining films.

March 18, 2007

LAST HOUSE ON DEAD END STREET (ROGER WATKINS, 1977)

A few years ago, when Barrel released their marvelous special edition DVD of *Last House on Dead End Street*, it was seemingly all that genre fans and magazines could talk about. There were many articles to read about the history of the film, production details, rumors, and a countless number of people claiming *Last House on Dead End Street* was the most disturbing film ever made. But for some reason, despite its welcoming into what could be considered a horror "canon," the initial wave of enthusiasm seems to have abated, and the film is now rarely mentioned. Originally released in May of 1977, this year, 2007, marks its 30th anniversary. Also, this year marks the sad death of its director, Roger Watkins, who, in addition to helming this film, was also responsible for several brilliantly atmospheric hardcore films made in the late 70s and 80s.

The plot of the film, at least in its extant version, is largely inconsequential to the grand guignol set pieces that give the film its reputation. In fact, it can more or less be summarized in a single sentence: Terry Hawkins gets released from prison and, mad at the world, decides to start making and selling snuff films to contribute to an ongoing acceleration sense of moral decay. Not surprisingly, that simple of a reduction overlooks everything that makes the film worthwhile.

The reason for the success & power of the film lies in the fact that it seems to exist in a void of pure, abject horror.

There are no characters in the film that one can empathize with as every character is wholly deplorable. Even Terry's victims are awful people; one male victim's wife, in an early scene in the film, gets dolled up in black-face before being performatively whipped while party guests laugh and clap in glee. This is the world that the characters are situated in. It's hopeless, dirty, and very bleak.

The idea that the narrative features an abundance of "plot holes" is most likely due to the fact that the only available version of the film is 74 minutes long, whereas supposedly, somewhere in a New York film archive, a 175-minute version is sitting. One cannot even imagine what exists in the other 100 minutes of film.

Nowhere else in cinematic history has such an abject void existed so successfully. Virtually everything that occurs serves to disorient, confuse, terrify or disturb the viewer. What really makes the film work so well are the small moments and aesthetic decision that serve no goal other than to bewilder the audience; the masks that Terry has his 'girls' wear during films, the fake head arbitrarily placed next to the head of a victim as she is dismembered, the dismembered deer-hoof that the producer is forced to fellate during his final moments. On their own, these elements serve as the merely bizarre, but an unexpected totality shifts these objects and displacements to a cohesive signification that something is *very, very* wrong. It is for this reason that the film is a success; it's a no-budget film that exists not within the realm of the 'so-bad-it's-good,' but rather as pure dejected atmosphere. The story isn't necessary; if all the viewer could see was the film with all overt narrative elements removed (dialog, narration), the exact same sense of affect would be achieved.

It may be very obvious that when Watkins made the film he was intending to play into the Manson phenomenon (particularly invoked by Terry's girls chanting things such as "Terry will solve everything, Terry will remove your fear"), as well as the conceptual idea of snuff that was closely linked to that incident. But what Watkins truly succeeds in doing is cinematically constructing the idea of something "other," something deeply terrifying to mankind. The unknowable "other," here, is a nihilistic snuff film director, and the nihilistic, utterly abstract content of his snuff films. And it is truly terrifying.

With the terror comes a sense of displaced beauty. The aforementioned signifiers that further separate reality from this filmic world are sublimely remarkable. The cheap but terrifying masks that haunt Terry's snuff films; the second fake head next to an actual victim; these images are separate from reality, a simultaneous sign-posting and disruption of the duplicity between reality and the image, and a deep-seated revelation that this film exists as its own reality, not connected to what the viewer considers the 'real world'.

While the film does suffer serious shortcomings in terms of plot, this is highly irrelevant to the success of the film. Undoubtedly if the plot were more cohesive the film might be more often discussed than it is today, something perhaps far more notorious and less experimental. But as it stands, *Last House on Dead End Street* is still a sublimely beautiful piece of atmosphere predicated upon desperation and nihilism.

May 18, 2007

LOST PARADISE
(MASAMI AKITA, 1990)

It may seem odd that I'm taking time to review what is ostensibly (from my understanding, at least) a fetish film. In fact, it may even seem counter-productive; fetish film (or video) rarely has any pretense beyond what it literally sets out to do: depict an extremely specific situation that someone is sexually interested in. The films and videos make no effort to appear to a general customer, rather they are tailored to the specific, niche audience that spends time waiting for the films that will fill their specific desires.

Lost Paradise was one of six seppuku videos produced by Right Brain Video in the early 1990s. I have no idea how they sold, whether or not they were actually intended to be sold alongside more general AV releases or if they were marketed as something like a specialty gore video (the early 90s was also the time when the infamous Guinea Pig movies got their start and notoriety). With that said, for the purposes of this review I will treat the film as a specialty fetish video.

What little plot exists in *Lost Paradise* can be explained briefly; the scene cuts back and forth between a woman in militaristic garb walking down a hallway and a man standing in front of a fire. After she walks down the hallway, the woman sits down and begins to partially disrobe, revealing the top of her panties and her breasts (which, from information I could gather, is a regular element of the "genre" of seppuku videos, which seems to lend credence to the idea of fetishistic intentions), and begins fondling her stomach. Eventually, she pulls out a knife. After partially wrapping it in cloth, she penetrates the left side of her stomach, pulling the blade all the way from left to right meridian. As the knife slowly progresses, following large sprays of blood, her innards begin to fall out while she moans in ecstatic pain. Eventually, she dies. A man walks into the room, starts shouting (the copy I watched was not subtitled so I'm unsure of any specific linguistic relevance), and then shoots himself in the head. After the camera lingers on the two dead bodies from above, a fade out occurs and we see a new woman, also in militaristic garb, carrying a whip as an older man crawls before her. Fade out to credits.

The whole thing lasts about 34 minutes, and really, doesn't amount to much on a surface level. The production values are amateurish; and by that I mean that you can literally tell that there is somebody behind the lens that you (being the viewer) are currently looking through. It is also not the type of work that could easily be championed by gorehounds; the video is very slow paced and the gore almost feels more symbolic than realistic.

But those things really don't matter to me; rather, it's something that the video got me thinking about that was interesting. As I was viewing the film as a fetish video (I suppose as opposed to a gore video), the whole idea of representation became particularly relevant. To the fetishist, it doesn't matter that the camera work is below par and the whole ordeal looks "fake"—what matters is that the idea that the fetishist is interested in is merely depicted. This operating structure found me considering the fabrication of the ideas in these videos—I would presume that those who make the videos have to more or less share the fetish themselves, at least for their videos to achieve any sort of notoriety within the intended target niche. So really, watching the video is like watching a process, and the result of that process; the concept becomes the structure and there is not really any level of "distance" occurring.

The music, done by the video's director Masami Akita (infamous noise musician Merzbow of course—the reason almost anyone has even heard of this specific video) perfectly echoes what is displayed on screen. It's interesting for me, as a fan of harsh noise music, to see what happens when an image is directly juxtaposed with this sound, as I often find the soundscapes themselves aid in negating any sort of mental visual image. The musical selections that Akita chooses are some of his subtler, "low grumbling" pieces, which while being more or less omnipresent throughout the video, crescendo and consciously insert themselves periodically throughout the duration, and it is through these moments that it becomes apparent that despite what most might think of the Merzbow project ("It's just noise"), Akita is truly an artist; he shows an utter understanding of how the sound he creates can emotionally function. Another thing that I found of interest was the ritualistic nature of the events, and then my reaction of placing ritual in a fetish context. It is very methodical and very planned. It's unfortunate that the videography is so poor, as it's easy to find a sublime beauty lurking within the ritualized space of artifice.

I should note, however, that there are elements of the film that went over my head. There are sequences of events at both the beginning and end of the video that I'm incapable of ascribing meaning to, due to either my lack of familiarity with symbols (whether cultural or fetish-based), or my incapacity to understand the brief moment of dialogue that's present. As such, I don't refuse the idea that the work actually has a larger meaning than what I can read it as here, but I have only my own experience with the film to respond to here.

As a film itself *Lost Paradise* is nothing special. Rather, it's as a process, as a moment of ritualised fetish, that the video transcends what it actually is and becomes something worth talking about. And because of that, because of the ideas that it confronted me with, I can honestly say that it's interesting.

May 24, 2007

GEMIDOS DE PLACER (JESS FRANCO, 1982)

Franco made *Gemidos de Placer* during a period of time he was working with Golden Films Productions. It was at this time that he had returned to Spain to make films, and for the first time in his career was more or less free to make the exact films he wanted. Unfortunately, this freedom was accompanied by smaller budgets than normal, but despite financial shortcomings it was a period of wildly personal, poetic films for Uncle Jess.

Gemidos de Placer ostensibly takes its inspiration from *Philosophy in the Boudoir*, a short work written by the Marquis de Sade whose themes Franco returned to time and time again throughout his long career. The events of the film take place in a single night, from dusk to dawn, with only five characters present for the film's duration. At the beginning of the film, Antonio (Antonio Mayans) brings his friend Julia (Lina Romay) to his house for a night of debauched sex. We learn that Antonio's wife Martine has just returned from a mental institution. While Antonio reveals he is intending to feed Martine's insanity and send her back to the institution she has just returned from, the erotically charged events of the night, which includes the sexually fueled death of the couple's maid Marta, finds the husband-wife rekindling their relationship in unexpected ways. Julia and Martine also, through the course of the night, develop a close relationship, and eventually decide to take their own actions against Antonio.

Despite being composed of little more than prolonged sex scenes, the film rises above mere titillation or even base eroticism. In constructing the film, Franco takes a seemingly Materialist/Structuralist approach. The film is made up of twenty segments of roughly equal duration, which is to say, the film consists of twenty four-minute takes. The camera lingers on the corporeal acts, using focus to draw attention to inanimate objects in the room, creating an intensely erotic rhythm to the film. The extended shots never get boring; by demonstrating a very careful understanding of composition and depth of field, the viewers' eyes never stop moving, taking in the pure beauty of the scenes that Franco has created.

And this film is indeed one of Franco's most utterly beautiful. Despite the aforementioned budgetary constrictions, Franco economically takes advantage of every inch of the space his characters inhabit—the actors move in such a deliberate way it can read as choreography, figures dancing across the space of the frame always predicated upon the sexual act. In the way the characters orient themselves in space, the villa itself becomes an all-important sixth character.

While I compared the technical intent to a simplified Materialist/Structural film earlier, in terms of content *Gemidos de Placer* shares more in common with the more poetic strain of the avant-garde, obliquely invoking even such canonical figures as Maya Deren (in the choreographic movement of the characters, the inherent eroticism built out of material objects), but built upon an erotic rhythm rather than symbolic intent.

Franco's avowed interest in Jazz and Free-Jazz helps us to read the way he lets the movement of characters, the shifting gaze of the camera, and the free-plucking of the guitar-based soundtrack collide with one another, creating a totality that delivers the emotional impact of the film. In its curation and communication of sensual experience, the film conveys an extreme sense of emotion, which, I imagine, is why many Franco fanatics claim it as one of his best works.

In fact, what is easily the best scene of the movie comes shortly after the murder of Marta, as Julia desperately writhes and wriggles on a bed while the sun is rising in a window behind her (the rising sun a repeating image throughout Franco's oeuvre). The score of the film swells and the rays of the sun highlights Marta's body as she corporeally gestures signs of eroticism. The image is hypnotic, and possibly the most beautiful thing that I've ever seen in a Franco film. The movement of the characters and camera, the lighting, the music, and the rhythm throughout all of this serves to create such an intense emotional tension and create a filmic experience that doesn't mimetically represent something that the viewer can empathize with, but rather postures a sense of affect so the viewer herself can *feel* something.

With all that said, the film at times can feel tedious, as simulated sex scenes honestly take up more than 3/4s of the film's runtime. I wouldn't consider it a shortcoming of the film itself (as I think the film exists in the exact mode that Franco wanted the film to exist), but if one is not in the right headspace to *give oneself over the film* it can be hard to maintain attention.

Despite what could be perceived as its flaws, *Gemidos de Placer* remains a key film in the Franco canon, expertly handling the themes of love, sex, and death that Franco returned to time and time again in his filmography. It is also a very articulate demonstration that Franco himself, often referred to as a hack in terms of technical prowess, is remarkably adept at handling all the elements that make film as a medium the amazing thing that it is. If you can surmount any predetermined resistance to soft eroticism and give yourself over to the experience of the film that Franco envelopes the sex within, I can guarantee a fully rewarding experience, potentially unlike anything else you've ever seen in a genre film.

June 14, 2007

LIVING (FRANS ZWARTJES, 1971)

Frans Zwartjes is a very idiosyncratic & extraordinary filmmaker. His films all seem to exist completely disconnected from the real world. While one can assume this is at least partially due to the fact that he almost exclusively shoots interiors, the few times that his camera deviates into the outside world his unique lens finds the world alien to expectations. I spent a weekend watching 14 of his films (thirteen shorts and one feature), and at the end I felt like I had barely escaped from the realm of the uncanny. While viewing a Zwartjes film one often gets the feeling that they're seeing something they're not supposed to be seeing, that their act of viewing is transcending simple voyeurism and actually attaining violation. And this is why Zwartjes is amazing.

Living was my introduction to Zwartjes, and to this day it remains not only my favorite Zwartjes film, but also one of the most powerful films that I've ever seen. The film introduces a simple concept: Frans and Trix (Frans' wife and muse) walk around the freshly-painted empty living room of the house they have just moved into. The two arrange miniature furniture on a floor plan, crawl on the floor, and aimlessly look around. This is the entirety of the action in the film.

What makes the film so powerful is the incredible atmosphere. There is a large series of windows on one wall of the room, but Zwartjes exposes the film so the panes are filled with nothing but a sublime white, totally removing the room from the outside world. For all the viewer knows, the house could be located in outer space. This detachment helps to enhance the idea of Trix and Frans in total isolation from the rest of the world. Zwartjes also shot the film with the widest-angle lens as he could find that didn't fully end up being a fisheye lens, and this decision extends the atmosphere of isolation that has already been established by the empty room and detached pervasiveness.

But despite its particular visual stylings, what truly brings the film together is the soundtrack. Discordant, errant organ chords permeate the viewer's ears as the ghostly-pale faces of Trix and Frans wander around their space. The soundtrack is some of the most hauntingly beautiful music that I have ever heard in my entire life, and the effect that the score has on the images is utterly remarkable; a testament to that inherent aspect of cinema, the marriage of sound with images.

Along with the uncanny mood of isolation, Zwartjes also manages to carry a remarkable sense of sexual tension in its editing. The pace of the majority of the film is calm and studied, but several scenes explode into hyper-quick & brief cuts of Trix' breasts and underwear as she lounges around the empty space. Zwartjes himself remains stoic in his hushed countenance, constantly biting down on a handkerchief as he continues to examine the space around him, occasionally stealing fetishized glances at his wife.

Gaston Bachelard, in his *Poetics of Space*, remarks that "[...] it [is] reasonable to say we 'read a house,' or 'read a room,' since both room and house are psychological diagrams that guide writers and poets in their analysis of intimacy." With *Living*, Zwartjes not only reads the room himself, but allows the viewer to do the same. Within the isolation, an obsessive relation between Frans and Trix is fully apparent. These rooms not only keep the outside world from spilling in, but also keep lust and obsession from spilling out.

Aside from everything else, it's worth noting just how accomplished & distinctly *his* Zwartjes' aesthetics are. By processing his own film, Zwartjes is able to push and pull his images: this lets him saturate his images in a way that wouldn't be possible without the explicit materialist intervention. The frame is permeated with blinding whites, grayish blue hues, the deepest greens, and, occasionally, a shockingly intrusive red. The color palate itself adds to the overwhelming abject sense of the uncanny in the most beautiful way imaginable. Not only are the colors wonderful, but the camera movement is an amazing feat in itself. All of the film is shot by Zwartjes himself while he remains in frame for most of the film. His shots are handheld, and he handles the camera in disorienting swooping motions so well; there's not a shake to be found.

It's no surprise, given the power of *Living*, that Zwartjes himself calls it his favorite. It's an unmatched examination of architecture and physical space representing a poetic emotional state, and it's a testament to a personalized sense of aesthetics.

October 18, 2007

DIRTY MARIA (TAKAHISA ZEZE, 1998)

Japan's pink film genre is endlessly fascinating to me. As an area of interest, it is seemingly ignored in the west, excepting occasions where genre fans view the films for the titillating aspects. Which can't be faulted, as even in their native Japan, the target audience for the pink film is almost the equivalent as the target audience of pornographic videos here in America; they are sold as sex films, and generally accepted as sex films. What is so fascinating to me is that in virtually all of the better examples of the form that I've had the opportunity to see, the films transcend being mere sex films in a remarkably potent way.

The genre shares many characteristics with films like *Through the Looking Glass* and the hardcore films of Roger Watkins; namely a sense of disillusionment, existentialism, and the loss of individuality. One will notice that these descriptors can also often be applied to canonical art house films like those of Robert Bresson and Ingmar Bergman. So why is it that these films are so easily dismissed?

The easy answer, of course, is that they're primarily sex films. They're low-budget productions, most often barely pushing feature-length (with run times almost always ranging between 55 and 75 minutes long), and often dogeared by genre critics as a primary example of Japan's "otherness." Aside from the intellectual conceits, which go virtually unmentioned by most, the genre is often painted as notorious for depictions of S/M situations, the abuse of women in power, and a supposed fetishistic attention to female nipples. While these elements are certainly present in many of the films, they are not always so simplistically par for the course. In the same way critics can't notice Russ Meyer's remarkably forward-thinking editing & political commentary behind the abundance of large-chested women, the emotional impact, development of affect, and thought-provoking ideas set forth in pink films are almost always rendered moot by some yahoo wanting to talk about how "sexually crazy" everyone in Japan is.

Of course, as I've already mentioned, it's these marginalized attributes that makes the genre so potent to me. I'll be the first to admit that not every film from the genre is a stunning example of what I've highlighted above; many are little more than poorly-made smut. But in an industry that cranks out hundreds of films every year, it'd be absurd to expect each and every one to be a masterpiece.

In the context of the films that work the best, the "otherness" present in the depictions of sex doesn't seem so off-putting—in fact, it's rarely presented a something outre for the sake of being outre. Often the violent or sadomasochistic sex works as a perfect extension of characterization and emotional states that are being played out on film; generally dramatic events are remarkably intense, and what is generally considered to be "normal" sex would be out of place. "Normal" sex wouldn't punctuate any of the films' action, intellect, or emotion; like any smutty late night cable movie in America, it would be titillation for the sake of titillation.

Takahisa Zeze is a director grouped in with the shitenno, or "Four Heavenly Kings." To quote Roland Domenig from his particularly perceptive article Vital Flesh: The Mysterious World of Pink Eiga, the films of the Four Heavenly Kings were notoriously "'difficult' — they had too little sex, and gloomy, complicated plots." Compared to the banal, generic examples of the genre, this is certainly a true statement. But that is why the films from the shitenno are remarkable works of cinema.

Zeze's 1998 film *Dirty Maria* is a wonderful example of the type of cinema that the Four Heavenly Kings are notorious for. It's difficult, emotionally charged, existential, very gloomy, and enigmatic. It's also an incredibly beautiful film, taking full advantage of the snow-covered, isolated spa that the second half of the film primarily takes place at.

The film begins by introducing us to the titular Maria who works as a secretary/maid (for want of a better word) at a beauty salon. She is mostly quiet and keeps to herself, going home at night to her naively happy husband and small child. We are then introduced to Murakami, a dejected taxi-driver. We later find out that his dejection is due to his search for his missing wife, Mayumi.

Maria has killed Mayumi. Whether out of jealousy, or something bigger, she kills Mayumi and cuts up her body, distributing the body parts in opaque black plastic bags to different dumpsters throughout the city she lives in. When Murakami comes to the beauty salon in a desperate attempt to find Mayumi, Maria informs Murakami that Mayumi had mentioned wanting to go back to a spa that she had visited on a company trip. Soon Maria and Murakami are in a car together driving across the icy expanse of abandoned roads, on their way to the nearly abandoned spa.

Once the characters are subtly established, the remainder of the film explores the relationship that Murakami and Maria develop as their own personal secrets are revealed to one another. There is no love or happiness in the relationship that our protagonists develop, but instead there is a sense of desperation and necessity.

As previously mentioned, the film is gorgeous. Ecstatically framed, snow-covered mountains fill the background while Maria and Murakami, both wearing striking red clothing, stand against the shockingly white snow, the contrast between the bodies and their surroundings forcing the viewer to associate these two disparate individuals as compulsorily linked. The visuals in the film also create an inexorable calm—there is never any superfluous movement in the frame, only the stoic environment and shockingly apathetic characters, excepting, of course, occasional tracking shots that are loudly striking in contrast to the static shots they follow.

In fact, much of the cinematography wouldn't be out of place in a Michael Haneke film; events beginning in the frame of the camera, then moving out of the frame while the camera stays still. There is also something genius about the hyper-literal use of an "icy" environment to help emphasize the "icy" detachment present in our protagonist's lives. The film is also almost completely devoid of dialogue; I would estimate that out of the 75 minutes that make up the films runtime, less than 15 minutes involve any dialogue.

But what is most rewarding and enigmatic about the film is Zeze's visual and narrative detachment. The motives of both Maria and Murakami are completely obscured to us as viewers. At no point in the film are we allowed access to the psychological state that initiated the actions that have been playing out throughout the film. We occasionally get vague insight, such as when Maria remarks, in regards to killing Mayumi, "It was surprisingly easy to kill her... because we die so easily."

Aside from the detachment that's present throughout the film, Zeze throws in abjectly odd, subtle events that heighten the atmosphere present. For example, in an early scene with Murakami driving his taxi, a customer gets in and begins asking Murakami if he's "ever done S&M," because he has just gone to a telephone club with somebody's wife. In the middle of the man's story, Murakami asks the man to get out of the car, as he's had enough of his job for the day. Aside from revealing Murakami's utter frustration with his disloyal wife, it also sets up the idea of giving up that permeates the ideas in the film. Another particularly pertinent example comes when Maria is having sex with her co-worker Sawai. As he pulls off his underwear and reaches for a condom from his jeans, she stops him, remarking, "we don't need that this time." There is an utter sense of futility in what she says, revealing that she too has already given up, she's no longer concerned with most of the world.

All in all the film is an intensely atmospheric window into characters who are emotionally empty, hanging on to whatever that they can grasp, going through life in a desolate trance, yet passively remaining in search of connection. As viewers, we are never met with a sense of closure to the events that we have been introduced to. Instead, we are bombarded with atmosphere and implications; we're asked to *feel* instead of to discover meaning.

October 26, 2007

VENUS IN FURS (JESS FRANCO, 1969)

The first time I saw *Venus in Furs* was years ago; Blue Underground's stunning DVD presentation had yet to be released, and with only six Franco films under my belt, I was still a Franco novice. I had been working through the few films of his that I could find via the bootleg trading circuit, and before *Venus in Furs* the only title that had struck a cord was *Virgin Among the Living Dead*—but my experience of *Venus in Furs* was something different. *Venus in Furs* was the first Franco film that I got truly excited about. After my first viewing on a crummy VHS dub I immediately rewound the ending credits and watched Barbara McNair's wailing voice calling out: "Venus in furs will be smiiiiiling—when that moment arrives..."

Watching the film now is a totally different experience. The film has changed—well, perhaps the film hasn't change, but the way I watch Franco's films has. In fact, my entire method of watching films has changed. If there's anything that writing about film has taught me, it's the importance of being an active film viewer. And often, with Franco's films, being an active film viewer requires you to watch the film within the context of Franco's larger oeuvre.

But I'll touch on that later, as I'm also a staunch supporter of the idea that a piece of art, if it can be labeled "good," should be able to stand on its own—and *Venus in Furs* certainly does. Franco has—throughout the many taped interviews that delightfully complement DVD releases of his films—shown himself to be a jazz fanatic; the music inspires everything he does. In the case of *Venus in Furs* this inspiration is obvious: the story follows trumpet player Jimmy Logan (James Darren, whose character was based off of musician Chet Baker) as he falls in love with Wanda Reed (Maria Rohm), a woman whom he believes he saw killed over a year ago. Jimmy is also in love with Rita (Barbara McNair), a crooning chanteuse in the nightclub he is employed in. Uptempo and almost psychedelic music courtesy of Manfred Mann fills out the film; there is more music on display here than dialogue, something that works to Franco's advantage.

Opening on a sunlit beach (featuring a fence that shares more than a passing resemblance to the infamous fence that populates many films in director Jean Rollin's oeuvre), the viewer is immediately introduced to a theme that pops up again and again in the "Franco canon"—the idea of the sea, of water, as the beginning and the end. This is a motif that pops up at the end of *Female Vampire*, as Countess Irina drowns in her bathtub; in *Sexual Story of O*, when Mario carries the murdered Odile into the eternally looming sea; in *Vampyros Lesbos* with Countess Nadine drowned face up in her swimming pool; Antonio at the end of *Gemidos de Placer*, the list is unending! And it was last night, upon another viewing of *Venus in Furs*, that I realized why this film works so well.

I think it works so well—and holds the highest priority among casual Franco fans—because of the fact that it is both a microcosm of the Franco universe and an excellent example of European Genre Cinema (Euro-Cult, Eurotrash, whatever term you prefer). And there's a reason for this—the productions that Jess Franco made with Harry Alan Towers were international co-productions; and as such, there were a number of creative decisions that Franco lost control over. But, unlike many cash-grubbing exploitation producers, Harry Alan Towers wasn't incompetent, so the collaborative results remain strong, and while they may not be the pure-Franco fever-dreams of the Golden Productions period, they are certainly good films.

"Time is like the ocean, you can't hold on to it..." muses Jimmy as he tries to take reign over the events in his life—the total chaos that is causing him such emotional distress. The distortion of time is hyper-present in the film: in an early scene, introducing the murder of Wanda at the hands of three perverts, a party is filled to the brim with people, but nobody within the frame moves except our pivotal characters, the extras decorating the lavish room are frozen in place, echoing scenes from Alain Resnais' brilliantly elliptical *Last Year At Marienbad* but creating something entirely different. Scenes cut back and forth between the past and the present, even occasionally jumping into what we can only assume is the future. Nothing makes sense to Jimmy as he wanders through the carnival in Rio, and the narrative structure of the film serves to hide the truth (at least, whatever truth there is to be told in a work of fiction) from the audience. We never know more than Jimmy.

The exploration of time and memory, played out via an occasionally melodramatic love story, calls to mind a quote from Jacques Derrida in Ken McMullen's 1983 film *Ghost Dance*:

> "Ghosts don't just appear, they come back. In French we talk of them 'returning.' Now that presupposes a memory of the past, that has never taken the form of the present. [The] theory of ghosts is based on a theory of mourning. In normal mourning, Freud says, one internalizes the dead, one takes the dead into oneself, and assimilates them. This internalization is an idealization, it accepts the dead. Whereas in mourning, which doesn't develop naturally—that is to say, in mourning, that goes wrong—there is no true internalization. There is [...] 'incorporation,' the dead are taken into us but don't become a part of us. They just occupy a particular place in our bodies. They can speak for themselves. They can haunt our body and ventriloquise our speech, so the ghost is enclosed in a crypt, which is our body. We become a sort of graveyard for ghosts. A ghost can be not only our unconscious, but more precisely, someone else's unconscious. The other's unconscious speaks in our place. It is not our unconscious, it is the unconscious of the other which plays tricks on us. It can be terrifying, but that's when things start to happen."

And things do indeed *happen* for Jimmy as he's haunted by the memory of a dead Wanda—a memory so strongly carried by love and lust that he seems to somehow corporeally manifest her. This manifestation becomes the catalyst for the events in the film. There is, of course, a subplot of revenge that plays out amidst the "romantic haunting," but in terms of cohesive "plot," it's hardly relevant. This diversion is, however, necessary to the success of the film. It is within this counter-plot that a strong portrayal of European Genre Cinema tropes surface, it is this subplot which balances out the "non-Franco" elements of the film, creating the dichotomy of the private film (Franco's "inner" methodology—at least when he has full control) and the public film (the idea of the "exploitation" film). This counter-plot is not merely empty genre-tropes to pad the runtime and sell to international markets, rather, this additional narrative presents an oneiric exploration of revenge, expanding Franco's musings on memory, ghosts, and regret. In this counter-plot, Wanda has returned to kill those who killed her, and it is no surprise when she discovers that all three of her soon-to-be-victims are still in love with their memory of her.

To further elaborate on the idea of *Venus in Furs* as a microcosm of Franco's oeuvre, one need look no further than the casting. Primary roles in the film are played by Maria Rohm, Klaus Kinski, and Dennis Price, all actors who pop up repeatedly throughout Franco's work. Part of Franco's brilliant intertextuality involves not only the repeated use of his favorite actors, but the repeated use of the same actors in the same archetypal roles. This idea adds to an inherent intertextuality of Franco's work, an intertextuality that helps compound multiple films into a more coherent cinematic *idea*.

But I digress—as I mentioned before, this is one of the few films from Franco's filmography that doesn't hold a total reliance on context to work. Aside from the literal content (narrative) of the film, much of the film's success is due to aesthetic or formal choices; specifically the photography and the soundtrack. As I've already mentioned, Franco uses Manfred Mann's music more than dialogue, and the tight, trippy, psychedelic jazz stylings lend a path for the fractured narrative to follow—this music is the metonymic pulse of the film's passion. And of course, what good would a European Genre Film be without striking visuals? It was 1969 and the peak of modern interiors are on display here, including a couple scenes shot inside Carlo Ponti's styled-up-to-the-minute house! Many of the party scenes wouldn't look particularly out of place in a Radley Metzger film, something rare for Franco seeing as his choices in art direction are generally far more sparse.

There are a few bits of post-production that lend an air of oneirism to the film at particularly pivotal moments. In deciding how potent these effects are, it's best to consider the film, once again, from both the private and public perspective: if viewed strictly as a Franco film, these oneiric events violate the fractured realism that seems to be driving the narrative (as Franco himself points out in an interview), however, viewing the film in the context of a "public" film (as an example of European Genre Cinema), it plays with genre tropes effectively. The special effects are not heavy-handed, serving only to highlight the intensity of the moments on display.

Whether viewed as part of the larger context of Franco's filmography or as a stand-alone genre film, *Venus in Furs* remains a brilliantly executed work, exploding with creativity and style.

January 22, 2008

ARREBATO
(IVAN ZULUETA, 1979)

As mesmerizing as its images are, what gives this film its power are the ideas that are present. The images are hypnotic, having what the film itself would describe as "occult rhythms," but without an idea behind the sublimity present in the incidents of super-8 film that populate the film, we'd be left with nothing but aesthetics.

There are several ways I would characterize my relationship to film: First and foremost, I am obsessive. Secondly, I find that a story works best (or is most interesting to me) when rooted primarily in abjection and the uncanny. I think abjection is an important term when considering this film. For me, the loci of abjection and the uncanny in cinema is met when genre film—particularly horror—intersects with the experimental. This is an allowance of the fantastic with an allowance of materiality, a performative necessity (as in the film itself is performing an act as we, the viewers, are watching), and an insistence that the qualities of film (image music text; movement, narrative) can achieve more than the inherent, assumed qualities of what the classical Hollywood narrative achieves.

Arrebato itself is at the threshold of genre and experimental cinema. Finding itself with one foot in both worlds, meshed together perfectly, it is a cinema of ideas, a cinema of power. It is a cinema of abjection. We'll start with this.

It's easy to turn to the theoretical construct—developed primarily by Julia Kristeva—of abjection when discussing the horror genre. A primary element of abjection is the idea of "letting go of something we would still like to keep."1 A dismembered arm, from the perspective of the amputee, is abject. Horror cinema is often a cinema of viscera: "blood, semen, hair and excrement/urine, we recognize these as once being a part of ourselves, thus these forms of the abject are taken out of our system while bits of them remain in our selves."

> According to Kristeva, since the abject is situated outside the symbolic order, being forced to face it is an inherently traumatic experience. For example, upon being faced with a corpse, a person would be most likely repulsed because he or she is forced to face an object which is violently cast out of the cultural world, having once been a subject. We encounter other beings daily, and more often than not they are alive. To confront a corpse of one that we recognize as human, something that should be alive but isn't, is to confront the reality that we are capable of existing in the same state, our own mortality. This repulsion from death, excrement and rot constitutes the subject as a living being in the symbolic order.

Arrebato is located in the space of abjection. Its narrative drive is the idea of the "rapture" (the literal translation of "arrebato"), a semi-mystical state of heightened being, a "pause," as Pedro, who is exploring this idea of the rapture, refers to it. When we are first introduced to Pedro, he does nothing but shoot film, an obsession that, we find out, helps him to keep from eating, sleeping, fucking, or shitting for prolonged periods of time. He lives in a state of hysteria, wildly crying as he watches the short fragments of film that he has shot. The only time he can calm down, the only time he can face the reality of humanity, is with the help of "dusty-dust"—heroin.

While the story of Pedro drives the narrative of the film, it is through the world of Jose—a filmmaker and heroin addict—that this narrative unfolds. Structurally, the narrative of Pedro is embedded within the narrative of Jose, until the end when the two threads collapse into each other (almost ontologically). As the film begins Jose is editing a film, a vampire feature that he is visually dissatisfied with. He arrives home from his apartment, after being gone two weeks for a shoot, to find his lover who had formerly left forever, and a parcel from Pedro containing a key, a reel of Super8 film, and an audio cassette.

Eventually, Jose sits down to listen to the tape, which retells the story of Jose's interactions with Pedro, as well as the development of Pedro's filmic alchemy. In his initial meeting with Jose, Pedro had recognized something special in him, something that indicated that Jose was an ally to Pedro's esoteric cause. While Pedro's haunted voice presents the idea that what it is that he can "see" is something mystical, it's obvious to the audience that the only thing that these two men have in common is an utter obsession with the cinema. As Jose remarks early on in the film, "It's not that I like cinema... it's cinema that likes me." In certain ways Jose is presented as an echo of real-world filmmaker Jess Franco—despite the fact he doesn't always feel satisfied with what he's doing, he suffers a pure compulsion to be making films. Pedro's obsession has already been explained, taking up literally all of his time. For better or worse, both Pedro and Jose are addicted.

This cinematic addiction is paralleled by Jose's relationship with Ana—his ex-lover. Their relationship, normal at first, quickly devolved into an empty state of living dependent upon heroin to keep it together. The heroin/relationship subplot helps to heighten the intensity of the film, the desperation present, as motivation for the film's denouement: a material example of obsession.

But now we must return to the idea of abjection: "The concept of the abject exists in between the concept of an object and the concept of the subject, something alive yet not." Let's consider re-writing this sentence as: What appears on film during the act of watching a film exists between the concept of an object and the concept of the subject, something alive yet not. Film's materiality captures a representation of a physical place, a physical person, an action that is literally happening. But what we see when we watch a film is not the actual physical place, it's not the real person, it's not the actual action: what we see is an image. What we see is neither live nor dead; rather, it's a representation of the image.

And this is what the film is about: *Arrebato* presupposes that film can be more than a representation—it suggests that film has power, and as Roberto Curti points out in his brilliant article on the film2, "the image of an object put on film does not share the same ontological reality as that of the filmed object." Eventually, both Pedro and Jose become nothing but film. They are no longer ontologically present in the physical, material world at the end of the film. Rather, they become pure simulacra—a copy without an original. They are ontologically filmic. The vampiric nature of the camera, brought to life through Pedro's "occult rhythms," has sucked people out of the "real world" (the diegetic world of the film) into an impossible "film-world."

It is through this ideological construct that a simple jump-cut removing an actor from the frame becomes terrifying. Obsession leads men away from the "real" world and into something else. A metaphysical afterlife that can be seen but not felt. Pedro knows that he is going to ostensibly "die" as the red pauses on his developed film become longer and longer, yet he prepares himself for and faces his "escape" with both desperate terror and an ecstatic insistence. There is beauty in the desperation, and we can feel it in all of Pedro's footage, the pulsing, rhythmic representations of the world moving at an intense tempo: the moon crossing the sky, a penis erecting with the air of flora in bloom, clouds erasing the blue of the sky with a mask of white, people moving through life, etc., etc. These images are cinema's pulse, the bloodstream that keeps it alive.

Arrebato itself echoes the ideas that it diegetically presents: the film itself holds power over the viewers, calling upon desperation and rhythmic images, coupled with a compelling storyline, to cull the viewer into an active trance-like state. It is mysterious, enigmatic, and compelling. It is purely invested in its status as a film.

June 21, 2009

The quotations within this review of *Arrebato* were sourced from the following:

http://www.artandpopularculture.com/Abjection
http://www.horschamp.qc.ca/new_offscreen/arrebato.html

BLACK GARDEN (DIETMAR BREHM, 1987-1999)

Black Garden is a sequence of six short films shot and edited by Austrian filmmaker and artist Dietmar Brehm between 1987 and 1999. It's one of the first works that I've seen in quite some time that has managed to excite me on such a specific level: Brehm's films here occupy a cinematic position that could be called the "zero degree" of the horror film. Instead of constructing a horror narrative out of characters, plot, etc, Brehm assembles found footage that he re-shoots ("pumps") on super-8 and 16mm film with footage he shoots himself into atmospheric invocations of terror. The films, each between 15 and 20 minutes long in duration, create a unique cinematic space that cannot be described, only experienced. The films operate with imagery taken straight out of JG Ballard's *Atrocity Exhibition*; Brehm re-shoots and combines pornography, bondage footage, visceral surgery documentation, images of aggressive snakes and scorpions.

In an interview, he refers to his films as "stories," which I find fascinating and also revealing. With the exception, perhaps, of *Macumba*, there is no linear narrative to be found in the work, no matter how hard one stretches what's available on screen. But these "stories" are a different sort of narrative; a narrative of movement and atmosphere, where images are used not in terms of representation, but in terms of the *affect* they impose upon the viewer.

Because the films are inherently experiential instead of representational, the idea of a straight forward "review"—discussing plot points, acting, etc—seems futile. Because of this, I'd like to present the series of notes I've taken on the six films that make up the sequence.

The Murder Mystery (1987/1992, 18')

I watched this years and years ago and found myself entirely bored by it—I remember very little about my experience other than the fact I specifically remarked that the soundtrack "didn't work" for me. This time around the soundtrack feels perfect: field recordings of a thunderstorm, rain, wind, occasional bits of children laughing. The film constructs something that can barely exist on screen, something that is rather hinted at through light and shadow—it's almost primordial in its construction. Yet, what is it hinting at? A sadistic sexual horror. This is horror film degree-zero.

Blicklust (1992, 16')

Bookended by shots of curtains billowing in front of windows, this is a film to be projected in the medical cinema within the diegesis of Ballard's *Atrocity Exhibition*. Similar to *The Murder Mystery* in its construction of affect via refusing to cement details, here we are provided primarily with both footage of visceral surgery being performed inside of a wrist and footage of a bored woman in soft bondage. Where in *The Murder Mystery* the terror is constructed by the cumulative outcome of how everything comes together, here it is the footage that lies outside of the dominant tone that ends up causing the most anxiety.

Party (1995, 17')

Not quite as successful as The Murder Mystery or Blicklust, but still carries a mood of simultaneous dread, ennui, trauma and anxiety. The most fascinating parts of this short is the footage of two scorpions fighting, the beautiful grain of super8 combining with the flicker of Brehm's "pumping" creating an unforgettable image.

Macumba (1995, 18')

In the matrix of experience, it seems that Brehm's films often derive meaning from their own titles. In this case, "Macumba" means "magic" and "witchcraft," two separate words that, in certain cases, carry the same meaning, but can often be considered to mean wildly different things. Witchcraft is often cast as "negative" in terms of its mode of generally being explained as an action upon (against) an enemy, and magic often positive, if considered in the connotation of, for instance, "Oh, what a magical evening!" And within this semantic tension, the film finds its point of departure. The terror present, or perhaps the anxiety, in the other Black Garden films is mostly absent here (unless, I suppose, the viewer is repulsed or terrified of snakes?)—instead there's a pulsing combinatory effect that ends up working differently than the other films in the sequence. The experience is much lighter: this is the first film in which we see close-ups of individuals smiling, whether in the anthropological footage or in the sex footage—in fact, the individuals on screen are *happy*. This makes me think of the second semantic inscription of "Macumba" above: magic, what a magical feeling. It's not inherently a happy film, as Brehm refuses that sort of experience in Black Garden, but rather there's a sort of airy ecstasy that floats through the duration. Similarly: the close-up super-8 shots of the cobra, "pumped" by Brehm, might be some of the most astonishingly perfect images of cinema.

Korridor (1997, 18')

Scribbled while viewing:
Spatial exploration / lens confrontation / the overwhelming dimension of sound / the interstitial moments of sexual perversity / panning over a constricted body / an unsettling insistence / corridor of the title = the lens itself / voyeurism, the violence of BDSM (both men & women receiving the violence) / complicit abjection / the construction of an 'underworld'

Another entity that occupies a unique realm of terror: with the footage Brehm composes, he creates a sort of space that echoes the feeling of a terrible "beneath." A space of perversity, where the image of terror is challenged regularly by the knowing complicity of the 'actors' involved. A man smirks, shirtless in bed next to a woman prostrate, not-moving. Is this a dead body? No, this is an image in a film, a found image reincorporated into a cinematic space. A beautiful terror, accompanied by a fragmented soundtrack that refuses as much as it inspires.

Organics (1998/1999, 18')

This is not only the strongest film in Brehm's Black Garden sequence, it's also a near-perfect film in its own capacity, as well as a perfect note to end the sequence on. As I was so taken by the film itself, I fear I have little to note here, though I did find a vertiginous sense of anxiety traveling through my body as the film unfolded before me on my screen. While some people fear heights for the corporeal sensation they experience before them, my body, and head, take that sensation and enjoy it, and that's what this film feels like.

August 12, 2015

PASSACAGLIA Y FUGA (JORGE HONIK, 1975)

I am struck by the silence that the sea presents, opening the narrative space. A film primarily shot inside the contrast between the silence (and, in terms of camera movement, stillness) of the sea with the at-times overwhelming natures of Bach's organ piece (which amps up in volume and intensity as the film progresses)—I'm not one to read for metaphor but this is a ripe comparison of internal vs external (and more appreciated on my part for its literal nature).

The beauty of the film, while certainly heightened by the quality of the images and the light, is obtained primarily in the fluidity of the movement, of the horizontal pans only occasionally interrupted by gestural significance (the breathing of a body, a spinning chalice, the blinking of an illustrated saint's eye).

John Lecht, in an essay on Bataille, states that "verticality can refer to the axis of transcendence, where transcendence refers to objectification, conceptualization, representation, distanciation, homogeneity, knowledge, history (as written or as narrative) and, more generally, to the domain of theory especially in the sense of theoria: to see. Horizontality, on the other hand, refers to immanence, and thus, secondarily, to ritual, difference, horror, silence, heterogeneity, abjection (in Kristeva's sense) and, more generally, to the domain of [the] nondiscursive, or practice." With this in mind, I'm always fascinated by how artists use each axis. Bernard Noël, himself a "disciple" (for want of a better term) of Bataille, subverts Lecht's explanation and insists upon the verticality of poetry on the page, the way it functions as a stake into the ground (or into a body), the way it stands upright.

Honik's horizontality sits somewhere between Bataille and Noël. The shots compress time in their tracking; the pans feel closer to ritual and difference (qualities which Lecht attributes to horizontality). I'd also insist that, in certain ways, despite being literally visual, revealing more of the space of whatever we're looking at, the tracking shots fail to truly allow us as viewers to *see* the space; when tracking over the spines of books we move too quickly to focus on any in particular; when tracking from left to right across the window upon the mountain we move through such extreme compression of time we can never see the present, only an overall impression of passing time and seasons. Our sight, in many ways, is obscured.

But with all that said, this film succeeds primarily in how it uses everything mentioned above in tangent with the increasing intensity of Bach's organ piece; the title cues us into this, lets us know to both expect and excuse a heavy reliance on music. Here the reliance on music does not predicate the way the film is cut (an incredibly smart move, for rhythmic intensity differs wildly from the sort of slow-building intensity that Honik matches to the organ here), but rather allows us to accept the swelling that at times threatens to push the limit, to overwhelm.

January 7, 2018

ESOPHAGUS (JAMES FOTOPOULOS, 2004)

This feature from Fotopoulos cements what his other films have really only hinted at: Fotopoulos, at least in some instances, privileges the experience of watching the film over a direct presentation of narrative or, any sort of push towards an empathetic response via characters, psychology, etc. This is an idea that I return to with regularity, and there are very few examples of filmmakers who work with this idea either with feature-length runtime or with any semblance of narrative. The intersection of this cinematic modality with narrative is something that I'm particularly interested in as it's a modality I aim for in nearly all of my own creative work (that is to say: narrative work that is an experience all on its own rather than being a representation of an experience).

There's little enough critical writing on experimental film in general (especially outside of academic writing), and it seems even more rare to find writing on work that truly crosses genres—most of the findable writing on Fotopoulos's work seems to locate the work specifically within the framework of the "cult" film, an ambiguous signifier of genre that tends to refer to something that, twenty plus years ago, would have popped up in Psychotronic Video Guide. Categorically, this often describes non-normative work where any extraneous details or element of confusion get written off merely as "weirdness" or "enjoyable incompetence" or (my least favorite term) "surreal." Due perhaps exclusively to his earlier feature *Migrating Forms*, comparisons between Fotopoulos and David Lynch are abundant. Maybe throw in another completely unfounded comparison to or description of something more palatable and "psychedelic," emphasize how "weird" the films are, mention that they are put forward as deathly serious but can still inspire laughter, et voila, you have any given review of a Fotopoulos film from the past decade. This isn't entirely surprising, as anyone deeply interested in experimental film is rarely interested in genre film (and, perhaps even more so, the opposite—at least academically). The common expectations, of each genre, are different. While there was a time, mostly pre-internet, where experimental and art house films that occasionally touched upon any sort of prurient material (read: nudity) was often sold alongside horror and sci-fi films in printed catalogs of bootlegs or imports, this more lead to much of the above semantic categorization (aka "this shit is weird check it out!") rather than any sort of legitimate engagement of varying forms.

But what about those few singular filmmakers whose work does manage to cross these boundaries, equally treading both sides without posturing efforts towards either? There's a rich history of these ulterior and often-maligned genres ending up lumped together due to, as mentioned, bootleg tape trading culture and the fact that both "cult"/genre films and experimental/avant-garde work exist "outside" the dominant hegemony of film-making (a surface level reason for this is that horror films, pornography, and experimental film all tend to privilege the spectator's response over any sort of inherent narrative or psychology in the film itself: these films actively want to affect the outside rather than staying self-contained). But, despite these comparisons, different modes of filmmaking require different modes of viewing. You can choose to view everything you watch in the same mode, sure, but you're most likely not going to end up appreciating anything other than what already fits specifically into the mode you've decided to take. This is true across everything: if your filmic expectations derive exclusively from watching commercial cinema, anything that falls outside of these parameters is ultimately not going to meet the expectations you have; if your filmic expectations derive exclusively from the pleasure one can derive from incompetent genre films, a film that competently explores ideas that are also found in said films is going to be met with the same sort of disdainful giddiness and not be taken seriously.

There's two sides to this, and honestly I'm equally open to both: the first side posits that you need to take each film on its own parameters without imposing a pre-existing framework upon it. Conceptually I think this is the best way to approach things, but nothing in the world, yet alone cinema, exists in a vacuum, so it's impossible to ignore systemic notions that creep into a work whether the artist intended such notions or not (for instance, just because a director isn't intentionally making a racist statement, it doesn't mean his film doesn't fall prey to perpetuating racist ideology, etc). This is inescapable. Similarly, because what is accepted as the "standard" mode of viewership is the mode that has been presented and dominated by commercial outlets (which, more recently, means the serialized "central conflict narrative" of this quote GOLDEN AGE OF TELEVISION end quote) it's not surprising that most people cannot escape their preconceptions and view a film outside of said parameters. Just because this isn't surprising doesn't mean that we should accept it, as it closes off many wonderful experiences to most audiences.

With all this said, I feel it necessary to point out that *Esophagus* is a singular work. Just as likely to alienate as it is to fascinate (possibly the same viewer in different head-space), the 2004 feature uses a variety of forms and mediums to create a unique space of despair. What it manages to do is literally carry a viewer through a hell-scape of extreme and dejected emotions. There's nothing to grasp onto, but even while you're grasping at air it sits as a film so incredibly powerful that I can't help but praise it.

Fotopoulos is regularly able to wrangle true gravitas out of scenes/acting/prosthetic or optical effects that lesser filmmakers would only be able to use in ways that result in failure: where Fotopoulos can produce something extraordinary, the same element in another film would either end up totally flat, ironically hilarious, or called out as a low-budget shortcoming. Fotopoulos warps these 'base' effects into an almost uncanny sense of abjection: prosthetic wounds that at first,—distanced in medium to long shots,—appear plastic and wholly artificial, close-up are revealed as grotesquely organic; bizarre appendages and body-horror pieces that wouldn't be out of place in cult-comedy take on an edge of pure terror; hyperbolically dramatic, emotional dialog is moved to pure depressive flatness by way of text-to-speech automation, somehow managing to elevate the bizarre dialog to a bizarre level of intensity.

One of the specific technical elements that Fotopoulos excels at is knowing how to make the most of the tools he is using, and using the right tools for his intentions. Shooting exclusively on film for the first decade and a half of his career, his transition to video in the 2000s strikes one as less a matter of convenience and more of a realization that video (especially primitive analog video) has untapped potential in the creation of zones of affect. While it's the combination of film and video here that add up to the space of experience Fotopoulos's film offers, it's arguably the video-photography that ends up feeling even more 'atmospheric' than the filmstock (literally not an easy task by ANY means, especially to me personally as someone who is inherently predisposed to preferring the look of low-gauge film over video).

The film is split into three major fragments, bookended by abstract photography, flickering screens of colors, indiscernible figures, the sound of the sea and a low hum. The footage used both at the beginning and the end of the film appears to be the same, but the experience of the footage is entirely separated by the "body" of the film in between. The footage, interstitial, sits as a boundary between the space of the film and the space of the world around you, and it's both a mechanism of transition—allowing your entrance into and exit from the film—and also a buffer space that literally allows the film to sit apart from the world at large. The film itself is impossible.

A simple rundown without much commentary:

- First section: nude women with grotesque, diseased wounds and growths have sex. Shot on film, faces and lines are scratched out on the celluloid.
- Second section: a group of men with bizarre growths and tumors adorning various bodily topographies wander around the space of an empty white room. All the men are dressed the same. Some of the men die. Some stare out a window, some sit on the floor. They

speak, but there is no diegetic sound; instead, a text-to-speech voice intones what one would assume is all of the dialogue in said fragment straight through four times in a row at different speeds.

- Final section: a depressed elf, a sex-worker, a young boy, and a man with a head injury are seen in various scenes inside an apartment. Once again there is no diegetic sound, only text-to-speech technology, but this time there are multiple "voices." The voices yell at each other, talk about depression, and in a final moment one voice tells the other of a place far away where everything is better, and that to get there you need the right group and weapons. The voices agree to go.

If there's any point of reference for this film, at least in tone, I can think of nothing other than Jason Hrivnak's writing; both *The Plight House* and his more recent novel *Mutilation Song*. I'm not one to insist on referentiality in terms of recommending something, but since Hrivnak's writing itself is somewhat obscure, the linkages here could speak volumes. This is not an easy film, rather it's an impossible masterpiece.

April 23, 2018

BLANCHE
(MARC HURTADO, 1995)

I have a difficult time writing about the films of Marc Hurtado due to how close they come to achieving what I consider a sort of platonic ideal of cinema. A personal ideal, for sure, but regardless, there's a complicated simplicity on display that carries virtually everything necessary for cinema to do what I want it to be doing, and with a degree of effortlessness. The elements: the body/the self, the sea, the way flora moves in the world, the gestures of man, light (above all light). There's more to it, of course, as these are indeed films, in all the medium-specific intensity said form indicates: they depend on movement, rhythmic editing, optical printing, light exposure, the hypnotic bent of duration, and sound, the wonderful sound of Hurtado's own Etant Donnes; sound intersecting with music, reacting to, with or against.

Before, in speaking of Kenneth Anger, I've drawn attention to the literal magickal workings Anger makes use of when combining music & film-image. The film-image sits on its own, silent, but the film in itself is not complete until sound begins to interact with it. If the magick works, the film-image and sound combine into a new sort of totality, driven by something other than the artists' direct hand, a confluence that lets interstitial chance (invisibly permeating the world) control the resulting outcome. This sort of near-alchemy is also practiced by Marc Hurtado, though his process is different from Anger's. In the case of Marc Hurtado, the sound-work is Hurtado's own sound-work instead of found music, sound-work that exists before the images exist. In conversation, Hurtado has told me that the film is not edited to the sound; rather, the film is edited first (in camera), and after the film-image sequence is complete, Hurtado introduces sound to the film without spending any insistence on editing the sound to fit the images. Hurtado says:

> "The music always exists before the images and I just put the music that [feels] good for each roll without cutting it, without any timing exercise and without [even] listening [to] it, it [is] only by magical grace[;] magic is the key of all these films."

The "magical grace" that Hurtado invokes is truly the key to his films. There's a moment about halfway through *Blanche* where a series of three cuts (arguably quicker cuts than most other places in the film, revealing a series of three singular images [in opposition to the density of the image present throughout the duration]) match up perfectly with the soundtrack: the synchronicity operates at a level that one would assume would have to be intentional, save for the fact that throughout the 32-minute film there are no other points where editing is tied so specifically to sound cues: as such the magical grace is perhaps most *literally obvious* here, as the collusion of sound and image envelopes the film in a sense affect away from any of Hurtado's own desire for control.

In fact, it's Hurtado's refusal to control, to dominate, his images that make the film work like it does, for the images and multiple-exposures are left up to chance as well. Again,

Hurtado states:

> "There [are] absolutely no edit[s] in these films, all the editing was made in the filming [...] when I needed a tree with flowers [and the same tree with snow within the same image] I just wait six months, putting out the roll and filming another roll [in the meanwhile].
>
> "It means that for each finish[ed] film it was 2 or 4 years of work [to have] the right mix of images, many times I [shot] 4 times each roll one over the other.
>
> "At one moment I [feel] that the film [is] finish[ed]..."

The process reveals a complete reliance upon this "magical grace," for if one is to watch virtually any of Hurtado's films made between 1976 and 1996 (the date range he ascribes this working method to) is to find an almost preternatural interaction of images, the world and the body, the inside and outside, the way images move together to indicate a larger idea of gesture or the world or, again, magical grace.

While I cannot, here, speak to Hurtado's intentions, *Blanche* very much seems to operate as a "conclusion" to both the aforementioned body of work, spanning 1976–1996, as well as a sort of "final statement" in the cycle of films that include *Aurore*, *Royaume*, and *Bleu* (the music from these films is tied to a trilogy; while I'm not positive, the sound Hurtado uses for *Blanche* sounds like an earlier Etant Donnes piece). The work that follows *Blanche* (and there seems to be a void of a decade between *Blanche* and the more recent films) has all been shot on digital video instead of film (with the exception of *Jajouka*, which Marc made with his brother

Eric Hurtado on Super16). While the work shot on digital video (especially the majestic *Le Saut* and *Ciel Terre Ciel*) have their own distinctive feel, in their examination of light the films reveal they share the same author as the earlier work.

Though, perhaps, this is beside the point. *Blanche* as a film stands alone, carrying such a range of potent intensity in its exploration of the figure, the gesture, the body, the world, the outside, a timeless place of magic, of holiness, of myth. The film speaks cosmic in using superimposition to flatten the sky to the ground, the sea to the stars: as above so below.

The final few minutes of the film, which seem like a coda in and of itself, features something distinctly separate from the work that has come before it (both the first 27 minutes of the film itself, as well as all of Hurtado's work which precedes *Blanche*): the nude body of a woman, an *other* apart from the body of Marc Hurtado himself. The use of the body remains unsettled: nude, but imaged in a way where there is a tension between eroticism and fascination, as if the camera isn't sure if the body is living or dead. Perhaps there's only a gesture here to recall the *other*, the male and female that create the use of nature [and I think this is more of a cosmic invocation than any sort of heterosexual impulse; the idea of reproduction in the world is predicated upon heterogeneity: *even flowers must be penetrated*]. The use of the female image becomes shocking, especially as the film refuses any sort of come down from the ecstasy it has spent a half-hour carrying: and this tension at the end of the film, in many ways, provides the only way out. A way into the world from the mythic and cosmic space of magical grace.

In ecstasy of the world.

July 13, 2018

www.ingramcontent.com/pod-product-compliance
Lightning Source LLC
Chambersburg PA
CBHW022023120726
47898CB00008BA/2615
* 9 7 8 1 7 3 3 5 6 9 4 6 0 *